ALICE
the Brave

BE SURE TO READ *ALL* OF THE ALICE BOOKS

"Naylor's funny, poignant coming-of-age series . . . has continued to serve as a kind of road map for a girl growing up today." —*Booklist*

ALICE
the Brave

PHYLLIS REYNOLDS NAYLOR

A Jean Karl Book

Aladdin Paperbacks

First Aladdin Paperbacks edition September 1996

Copyright © 1995 by Phyllis Reynolds Naylor

Aladdin Paperbacks
An imprint of Simon & Schuster
Children's Publishing Division
1230 Avenue of the Americas
New York, NY 10020

All rights reserved including the right of
reproduction in whole or in part in any form
Also available in an Atheneum Books for Young Readers edition
Designed by Michael Nelson
The text of this book was set in Berkeley Old Style.
Printed and bound in the United States of America

20 19 18 17 16 15 14 13 12

ISBN 0-689-80095-9 (hc)

Library of Congress Catalog Card Number: 96-85611

ISBN 0-689-80598-5 (Aladdin pbk.)

For Corie Hinton, with love

CONTENTS

ALICE
the Brave

Hang-ups

A month before I started eighth grade, I knew I was going to have to face something I'd been afraid of for a long time.

Everybody's afraid of something, I suppose–elevators, dogs, planes, spiders. . . . Up to this point, though, I'd steered around it. Made excuses. But when Pamela and Elizabeth, my two best friends, said we were going to spend the rest of the summer practically living in Mark Stedmeister's swimming pool, I knew I had to face my terror of deep water.

"I am going to tan like you wouldn't believe!" said Pamela.

"I'm going to perfect my back stroke," said Elizabeth.

Not even Dad and Lester, my brother, knew how frightened I was at the thought of water up over my head. When we went to the ocean, I never went out in water more than waist deep. Hardly anyone else did either, of course, so that was okay. And up until now, whenever the kids gathered at the Stedmeisters' pool, one of Mark's folks was always at poolside as lifeguard. I'd sit on the edge of the shallow end and laugh at the guys kidding around over by the diving board, and no one bothered me.

But now I guess they figured that since we were going into eighth grade, and Mark is bigger than his father, even, the boys could take care of any emergency. Mrs. Stedmeister looked out of the window a lot, I noticed, but she didn't sit out on the deck the way she used to, so we didn't have to wait for her to come out, or for Mark's dad to come home at night before we could swim. We had the pool to ourselves, and that's what made it so scary. That, and the fact that Patrick, my boyfriend, was up in Canada and wouldn't be home till the end of August.

The more time we spent at the pool, the bolder the guys got, and last time, after a lot of whispering, they'd all descended on Pamela. They'd picked her up in her pink bikini and tossed her into the deep end. Pamela did just the right amount of shrieking and flailing before she swam gracefully over to the edge and climbed out.

Of course, there are problems being Pamela, too. She used to have blond hair so long she could sit on it. When she was in the swimming pool on her back, her hair would spread out around her so that she looked like a goddess on a lily pad.

Then last spring, Brian put gum in her hair, and the only way she could get it out was to cut her hair. Now she has a short feather cut, and looks even older and more sophisticated than ever.

She doesn't always feel that way, though.

2

"I just feel so naked," Pamela said forlornly as we were coming back from the pool one afternoon.

Elizabeth glanced over at the bikini that barely covered Pamela's bosom. "Well, *look* at you!" she said.

Elizabeth wears a sort of halter-top suit that comes up high at the neck and is low cut in back. I guess she figures if she's modest in front she can afford to let go a little behind. She only worries about the part she can see.

"My head, I mean," Pamela said. "Sometimes I can still feel my hair, you know?"

"What?" I said.

"It's as though it's been amputated," Pamela explained. "Like a man who's lost a leg and can still feel pain in it."

"Pamela, that's spooky," I told her.

We were all feeling a little spooked, if you ask me. We had hardly finished congratulating ourselves on having survived seventh grade, and here we were, about to be eighth-graders. We had spent the last year envious of all those gorgeous, sophisticated eighth-grade girls we'd seen in the halls at junior high, and suddenly *we* were the eighth-graders!

Except that we didn't feel gorgeous or sophisticated, either one. I was feeling scared about Mark's swimming pool, Pamela was feeling amputated, and Elizabeth was as nutty as ever about bodily functions. We were as ready for eighth grade as we were for an earthquake.

Maybe, out of the three of us, Elizabeth was the most frightened of going back to school in the fall. She'd been shocked the way the eighth-grade girls leaned against their lockers sometimes and kissed their boyfriends—a long series of little glancing kisses on the lips—and she must have thought she was going to be required to do a certain amount of it before she graduated, I'm not sure. But I did notice that as July turned to August, she'd begun using the word *sex* instead of *mating,* and that was a step up. When she mentioned the subject at all, that is.

*Every*thing was changing, not just us. Lester was going to be twenty-one in September, and Dad just got back from a music conference in Michigan, where he'd gone with my English teacher, Miss Summers.

I had a million questions to ask him as soon as he got in the house.

"Have a good time?" Lester wanted to know.

"Did Miss *Summers* have a good time?" I asked, getting right to the point. I want so much for Dad to marry her that I even practiced writing my name Alice Kathleen Summers before I realized that if she married Dad, *she'd* be a McKinley, too.

"We *both* enjoyed ourselves," said Dad.

"How were the beds?" I asked.

Dad raised one eyebrow as he sat down on the couch and began taking things out of his briefcase.

"*My* bed, on the men's floor, was fine, Al," he said. (He and Lester call me Al.) "I don't know how Sylvia's bed was. I didn't ask."

Even though Dad says I can't ask him intimate questions

about him and my English teacher, I manage to find out what I want to know.

"I wonder if she packed that black sexy slip with the slit up the side that I saw her buying at Woodies," I said to no one in particular.

"I didn't ask her that either," said Dad. He frowned at me and smiled at the same time. "Watch it, Al."

"May I ask just one personal question?"

"No."

"That means you *did*!" I said, clapping my hands.

Dad was beginning to look exasperated. "That means nothing of the kind! Now see here, Alice . . . !"

"The question was, 'Did you hold hands?'" I said, grinning. I know how to get Dad's goat.

"We did on occasion hold hands, Al. Satisfied?"

"Then may I ask just one more personal question?"

"No!"

I clapped my hands again. "Then you did, you *did*!"

"*Al!*"

"Let's just say they made sweet music together," said Lester, and Dad said he'd go along with that.

Everyone is musical in my family except me. Dad said that when Mom was alive (she died when I was in kindergarten), she used to sing a lot. Dad plays the piano and flute, and he's manager of the Melody Inn, one of a chain of music stores. Lester sings and plays the guitar, and my English teacher sang alto in the *Messiah* sing-along. That's where Dad met her. Even Lester's girlfriends sing.

I can't carry a tune, so I don't sing at all except to myself, and only when I'm running the vacuum sweeper. Maybe I have a genetic defect or something. Dad says I have other fine qualities, though, and Patrick, my boyfriend, who plays the drums, says I have a good sense of rhythm, so I'm not a total loss.

After that little conversation with Dad, I was pretty quiet because I was thinking how the next five weeks were going to be absolutely awful. The one thing I would *not* do is tell Lester about my deep-water fear, because he would probably follow me to the pool and throw me in to *make* me swim.

"Anything wrong, Al?" Dad asked at dinner. I realized I'd got halfway through my chicken salad without saying a word.

I shook my head. I tried to think of something interesting to tell him and Lester to make them stop looking at me, but my brain went on hold. I could tell right away that Dad thought I was feeling left out because he wouldn't answer my personal questions about his weekend with Miss Summers, so he proceeded to tell me all the *impersonal* things they had done.

"It was sort of fun living in a dorm," he said. "Made me feel like a college man again."

"What'd you do? Streak across the campus naked?" asked Lester. Lester has a thin mustache above his upper lip, making him look a lot older than he is—old enough to have done any daring thing there is to do at college.

"No, we all went to the cafeteria each morning, then

Sylvia and I got in a mile walk before the seminars began," said Dad. "In the afternoon we practiced with the group of our choice and performed for each other in the evening. It was just plain fun! Sylvia even took a class in flamenco dancing."

I imagined my English teacher doing a Spanish dance with a rose between her teeth. I imagined us both together, she and I, dressed in Spanish costumes doing the flamenco together, beside a pool or something with everybody clapping. In my mind's eye, however, I danced a little too close to the edge and fell in, never to be seen again. I sucked in my breath.

Dad stopped talking and looked at me strangely.

"Hiccups," I said.

"Well, here's a little item that might interest you, Al," Dad told me. "Guess what you and I are going to do?"

"The flamenco?" I said warily.

"We're going to go shopping one of these days. I've decided it's time to get some new furniture."

"We already got a new couch," I told him.

"Not just a couch. Now that you're going into eighth grade, I think it's time you had a real bedroom set–dresser, chest of drawers, the works. Whatever you want."

"Dad!" I yelped, and leaned across the table to hug him. I hadn't the foggiest idea what kind of furniture I wanted. Not canopies and ruffles, like Elizabeth has, or the Coca-Cola logo in Pamela's room. Something that would reflect the real me.

"We need some new dining room furniture, too," Dad went on, and he and Lester began discussing whether we needed a table that would seat eight or ten. Something told me that Dad wasn't just doing this for me or Lester or even himself. He was doing it because he wanted a house Miss Summers would like to live in.

I studied Dad's face, looking for clues as to whether or not he might have proposed to her while they were in Michigan. No, I decided, he would have told us if he had. But he was sure getting ready for something big. He'd fix our house up first, *then* ask her.

It's stuff like this, I guess, that makes me nervous—where it's not just what you do that makes a difference, but what someone else decides. I could stay away from deep water for the rest of my life and do just fine, but what if someone threw me in? Dad and Lester and I could buy new furniture for every room in our house, but what if Miss Summers still said no?

It helped that Pamela had invited Elizabeth and me for a sleep-over that evening. The hardest thing about having a secret fear is keeping it secret, and I was afraid if I stayed around home that night, Dad would worm it out of me somehow. He'd go right to the phone and sign me up for swimming lessons at the Y, and I'd be petrified.

Way back in my brain I have this memory of someone taking me to swimming lessons. There was a tall skinny instructor in a gray bathing suit who threw rubber-coated horseshoes into the water. The deal was that when she said go, we were supposed to see who could jump in the water and pick up a horseshoe first.

I jumped in, but all I remember was the way I coughed and gagged as the other kids splashed around. I never did put my head under. The next time I went for a lesson, I wouldn't even go in the water, and then I didn't go back at all. Maybe that was about the time Mom got leukemia, and I suppose after that, the fact that I was afraid of the water was the last thing on anyone's mind.

Life is never perfect, I thought, as I rolled up my pajamas and stuck them in my overnight bag. Maybe all the gorgeous girls we were so envious of last year had secret worries, too. Maybe all the while they were leaning against their lockers, looking into their boyfriends' eyes and kissing, they were worrying about things like mating and jumping off the deep end. Maybe mating is like jumping off the deep end. What did we know?

I went across the street to get Elizabeth, and then we walked to Pamela's. We hadn't been spending the night much at Elizabeth's. Her mom's expecting a baby in October and still throws up in the morning, which is not exactly the kind of thing you want to hear while you're eating your pancakes.

In fact, this was the first time we'd been together over night since the three of us went to Chicago to visit Aunt Sally, and Pamela got groped on the train. Elizabeth was shocked that a man made a pass at Pamela, and then she was embarrassed because she was shocked. For Elizabeth, with the beautiful dark hair and long eyelashes, life is going a little faster than she wants it to, and she has to take giant steps now and then to catch up.

"My folks have gone to the movies, so we have the house to ourselves," Pamela told us at the door.

She has this incredible room that looks as though it were decorated by Coca-Cola—bedspread, drapes, waste-basket . . . When you lie down on her bed and the springs squeak, you almost think you can hear Coke fizzing somewhere in the background.

We played cards for a while, ate pizza, and then Pamela brought out this bottle of stuff that's supposed to make your hair shiny, and we practiced putting it on each other's hair and brushing two hundred times. We'd start to brush, but then someone would begin talking and we'd lose count and have to start all over again.

"Isn't Glo-Shine what they advertise on TV—the girl with the shiny hair and all the boys around her?" I asked.

"Sort of like lightning bugs," said Elizabeth. "One starts flashing, and they all gather round." Elizabeth can be funny when she wants to.

The strangest thing happened, though. As we were all brushing, Pamela must have forgotten what she was doing, because her brush slipped down past her chin, onto her shoulder. She absently brushed her shoulder, the way she used to do when her hair was long. She *did* have an amputation syndrome!

We were debating whether to watch the late movie or go to sleep, when Elizabeth said, "Listen, you guys. I brought something over . . . I thought maybe . . . well, maybe I could read parts of it to you."

She was sounding pretty mysterious. I'd never seen her quite that way before. Her face was pink, the way you look when you get out of the shower.

"What is it?" asked Pamela.

"Something I found on my parents' bookshelf."

I could feel my eyes opening wide.

"Do they know you have it?" Pamela asked.

"N-no. But it was right there. I mean, anyone could have taken a look. I've got to get it back by morning, though. I don't want them to find it's missing."

"What *is* it?" asked Pamela.

"A story." Elizabeth opened her bag and pulled out something wrapped in a pillow case. I took a look. *Tales from the Arabian Nights,* it read on the cover. *Unexpurgated edition.*

ABYSSINIAN SOBBINGS
AND OTHER STUFF

To tell the truth, I'd always thought that *Arabian Nights* was a movie. Maybe I was getting it mixed up with *Aladdin* or *Lawrence of Arabia,* but here was this thick book that Elizabeth put on the bed in front of us, and if you looked closely at the cover, you saw that this man was surrounded by half-dressed women, and the places they had their *hands* . . . !

"Have you read it?" I asked, truly astonished.

"P-parts," said Elizabeth.

"All the good parts, I'll bet!" Pamela said, smirking.

"It's a *story*!" Elizabeth said again. "Well, it's a lot of stories, really, but one of them is about this sultan whose wife is unfaithful, so he kills her, and then he kills all his slave girls and concubines and . . ."

"Wait a minute," I said. "He kills his wife because she's unfaithful, and he's got concubines?"

"Well, this was long ago," Elizabeth said. "Anyway, he ordered his vizier to . . ."

"His what?"

"His servant, Alice, to bring him a new slave girl every night, and then in the morning he'd kill her, and finally there weren't any girls left except the vizier's daughters. One of them, Scheherazade, had collected a thousand stories, so she begged her father to let her go to the sultan and somehow she'd stop the killing. The father let her go, and each night she started telling a story but never finished it, and the sultan got so interested that he'd keep her alive the next day, and then she'd begin another story, and finally the sultan didn't want to kill her or anyone else."

"So?" said Pamela, still looking at the book. "What are these people doing on the cover?"

"That's . . . that's what I was going to read to you," said Elizabeth.

Pamela and I hopped into bed like two little kids waiting for our bedtime story. We heard the Joneses come home and turn on the TV downstairs, but we waited patiently while Elizabeth pulled a chair over by the bed, turned on the lamp, and placed the book on her lap. It was then I noticed she'd put paper clips on some of the pages. She began reading:

". . . And as we were about to take ship again, we found on the beach a damsel in tattered clothes, who kissed my hand and said to me, 'Oh, my lord, is there in thee kindness and charity? I will requite thee for them.' Quoth I, 'Indeed I love to do courtesy and charity, though I be not requited.' And she said, 'Oh, my lord, I beg thee to marry me and clothe me and take me back to thy country, for I give myself to thee. Entreat me courteously, for indeed I am of those whom it behoves to use with kindness and consideration. . . ."

"What does she mean?" I asked.
"A virgin," said Pamela knowingly.
"Oh," I said, and Elizabeth continued:

". . . and I will requite thee therefor: do not let my condition prejudice thee.' When I heard what she said, my heart inclined to her. . . . So I carried her with me and clothed her and spread her a goodly bed in the ship and went in to her and made much of her. . . ."

I looked at Elizabeth. Her cheeks were pink, but she was already searching grimly for the next paper-clipped page.
"Is *that* all?" asked Pamela.
"Don't you have any imagination?" Elizabeth shot back.
I'll admit I was intrigued, but Elizabeth was already on to something else.

". . . So the damsel took a sash of Yemen stuff and doubled it about her waist, then tucked up her trousers and showed legs of alabaster and above them a hummock of crystal, soft and swelling, and a belly that exhaled musk from its dimples, as it were a bed of blood-red anemones, and breasts like double pomegranates. . . ."

I tried to imagine double pomegranates, whatever they were, and wondered if my breasts would equal even one.

Elizabeth's fingers fairly flew to the next paper clip. Pamela and I were having a wonderful time, but Elizabeth had the look of a girl waiting for the dentist:

". . . She put her hand into his breast, and it slipped down, and her entrails quivered and desire was sore upon her, for that women's lust is fiercer than that of men, and she was confounded. But when he never moved, she took his ring from his finger and put it on her own and kissed his mouth and hands, nor did she leave any part of him unkissed. . . ."

"Even his . . .?" said Pamela.
"Shut up, Pamela," I told her, and Elizabeth continued:

". . . after which she took him to her breast and, laying one of her hands under his neck and the other under his armpit, fell asleep by his side."

I was still concentrating on the quivering entrails, but

Pamela was clearly impatient: "It's nothing but foreplay," she said.

"It's what?" asked Elizabeth.

"What you do before you have sex," said Pamela.

"How do *you* know so much about it?" I asked her.

"My father subscribes to *Playboy*," said Pamela.

Elizabeth and I fell silent in the presence of such wisdom.

"Well, do you want to hear anymore or not?" Elizabeth said, and looked so ready to close the book that we had to beg her to keep going.

"I'll only read one more thing," she declared. "This is the last:

"The damsel told Noureddin to spend thirty of the dirhems on food, wine, and flowers, and the rest on silk of five colours. She cooked the food and ate and drank with him, entertaining him with talk and wine till he became drunk and slept, then arose and fashioned a beautiful girdle of the silk. When this was done, she removed her clothes and, lying down beside him, kneaded him till he woke and, finding beside him a girl like virgin silver, did away her maidenhead. They enjoyed each other that night with Cairene motitations, Yemani wrigglings, Abyssinian sobbings, Hindi torsions, Nubian lasciviousness, Rifi leg-liftings, Damiettan gruntings, Upper Egyptian heat, and Alexandrian languor."

Elizabeth stopped reading, and her cheeks were as red as the Coca-Cola logo on Pamela's wastebasket. From the look on her face, she was still mulling over the maidenhead, but I was struggling with the Yemani wrigglings, while Pamela had probably progressed past the Abyssinian sobbings and was all the way to Upper Egyptian heat.

There was an embarrassed silence in the bedroom. Obviously, there were whole categories of sexual conduct we knew nothing about.

Pamela must have been thinking the same thing. "Do you suppose they teach it in eighth grade?" she asked.

Maybe those gorgeous girls we saw flirting with their boyfriends in the halls had already taken the course, and the ones who spent their lunch hour in the library hadn't. Or maybe the ones in the library were reading *Arabian Nights*.

"I guess we won't know till we get there," I said. I was still amazed at Elizabeth. So was Pamela, and we watched her as she snapped the book shut, stuck it back in her overnight bag, her face still burning.

Reading from *Arabian Nights* didn't come easy for her. In fact, it was probably as hard for Elizabeth as swimming in deep water would be for me, because her own life was about as far from *Arabian Nights* as you could get. At Elizabeth's house, when you go in the bathroom, for example, there's a little decorated box with a lid that holds the Kotex. Everything personal is tucked away out of sight. No wonder Elizabeth went through that spell once of not being able to eat in public—in front of boys, anyway. A girl who pretends she doesn't sweat, menstruate, or go to the bathroom could hardly be expected to swallow and digest.

But on this night there was something else about Elizabeth that seemed different, and then I realized what it was. She was angry. Angry at Pamela and me.

"What's the matter, Elizabeth?" I asked finally as she plunked down her shoes and pulled a short gown over her bra and pants.

"Nothing," she said, and stomped off to the bathroom to brush her teeth.

When she came back, Pamela said, "Well, if you're not mad at us, you're mad at your shoes. You've kicked them out of the way three times."

"Why should I be mad?" Elizabeth answered. "You've been after me for as long as I can remember to be more . . . more *vulgar,* so now I was vulgar and I hope you're satisfied."

"Vulgar?" I said. "Elizabeth, all we ever tried to get you to do was to lighten up a little about bodies and sex without having a spaz every time we mentioned it."

"Well, okay, I've lightened up, so don't say I never talk about sex. I talked enough about sex tonight to last all year, so just shut up."

She turned out the light and crawled onto the cot over by the wall, leaving Pamela and me in the double bed.

Elizabeth meant it, too. I knew that she felt she had earned enough points to last her the whole of eighth grade, and she wouldn't have to say the word "sex" again until the start of ninth. But the real problem, I knew, was that she felt guilty about sneaking that book over here and was blaming Pamela and me for it.

The room was quiet for a long time. Then Pamela giggled. "Alice, what do you suppose Nubian lasciviousness is?"

"Oh, stop it! Just stop it!" came Elizabeth's voice over by the wall. "Can't we forget about it now and go to sleep?"

It was hard to sleep, though, with all *that* on my mind. I waited another half hour to see if I was getting drowsy. Pamela started snoring, and I figured Elizabeth was either asleep or she wasn't speaking anyway, so when I was sure the Joneses were out of the bathroom, I got up for a drink of water.

In a magazine rack in the corner was a copy of the July *Playboy*. I stared at the beautiful woman on the cover and was as curious as anyone else to see how she looked naked, so I opened the centerfold.

There was the girl stark naked, sitting with her arms close to her sides so that they sort of pushed her breasts together. Everything looked rose-colored, as though she'd just come out of a hot bath. Her cheeks were flushed, and her hair had little ringlets at the temples. Would I ever look like that without my clothes? I wondered. Not in my wildest dreams.

Not one of us mentioned *Arabian Nights* the next morning. Mrs. Jones had cinnamon toast and fresh orange juice for us, and Mr. Jones came to the table looking very ordinary, with his hair thinning a little on top. I was tempted to say to him, "How did you like Miss July?" but I didn't. Maybe you don't call the Playmate of the Month "Miss" anyway. Besides, ever since Pamela told me that her parents were nudists, I never quite knew what to say to them in the first place.

It was on Thursday night, when Dad was getting ready to do the grocery shopping, that he stood at the door looking over the list and called, "Who wrote pork sausage? How much do you want?"

"I did, Dad. Make it a couple packages, will you?" said Lester.

Dad jotted down something with his pencil, then scanned the list again.

"What's this? Double pomegranates?"

I swallowed.

"This your writing, Al?"

"Yeah. Pomegranates," I said.

He looked at me strangely. "Do you suppose a couple will do?"

"Yeah, two would be perfect," I told him. "I just want to see what they look like."

3

Waiting It Out

"Alice," came Pamela's breathless voice over the phone the next day. "I'm not going to Mark's this afternoon. Don't tell anyone, but I'm meeting Donald Sheavers at Wendy's at two."

Donald Sheavers is my old boyfriend from Takoma Park. Elizabeth and Pamela and I had met him recently at the mall, and he'd asked for both their phone numbers. I was just glad to have him interested in someone besides me. Donald Sheavers is one of the handsomest guys I ever saw, but he's also rather stupid. He can't even begin to compare with Patrick.

He *had* grown a lot larger than he was in fifth grade. I think Pamela liked his muscles, and Elizabeth was attracted to both the muscles and the cross he wore around his neck. But Pamela was supposed to be Mark's steady!

"Pamela, someone's bound to find out sooner or later," I told her. "What if Mark hears about it? You should tell him yourself."

"Well, Alice, how do you know if someone's right for you if you never go out with anyone else?" she said. "Donald's just . . . interesting, that's all."

"Okay, I won't mention it to Mark," I said.

"Or Elizabeth, either."

"We promised to tell each other *everything*!" I was one to talk. I'd never even told Elizabeth and Pamela how afraid I was of Mark's pool.

"Well, let me see first how things go. Then I'll tell her myself," Pamela said.

I had scarcely finished reading the comics before the phone rang again.

"Alice," came Elizabeth's voice, and it sounded as though she didn't want her parents to hear. "I won't be going with you and Pamela over to Mark's."

Oh, no.

"Listen, don't tell anyone, but Donald Sheavers called, and he wants me to meet him at the Orange Bowl at three o'clock."

Elizabeth was meeting a boy in *secret*? Obviously, Donald Sheavers was going to have lunch with Pamela and dessert with Elizabeth. I decided to stay as far away from the mall that day as I could get, and since neither Pamela nor Elizabeth was going to Mark's, I could stay home.

"Have fun," I told Elizabeth.

The really nice thing was that I got a postcard from Banff. It was from Patrick. The picture on it looked like Switzerland:

Hi, Alice,

Bet we're cooler up here than you are—unless you're in Mark's pool right now. We hiked in the woods today, and tomorrow we're going to walk around on a glacier. Only you have to be careful not to fall in a crevasse. See you in a few weeks.

Patrick

I wished he'd said a little more. I suppose he didn't want to put anything too personal on a card, but even if he didn't sign it "love," couldn't he at least have called me "dear"?

When Dad came home from the music store that night, I said grumpily, "Why don't we ever go hiking on a glacier?"

Dad gave a loud sigh and hung up his sport coat. "Al, an order of sheet music didn't arrive today, and two of my instructors didn't show. It's been a rough afternoon. Don't bug me." And he sat down to look over the mail.

I waited awhile and then said, "I got a postcard from Patrick. They went hiking on a glacier."

"Good for them," said Dad.

It was my turn to cook, so I went out in the kitchen and opened a jar of tomato and mushroom sauce, then boiled some spaghetti. By the time I'd melted butter for the garlic bread and made a salad, the kitchen was beginning to smell pretty good. I looked up to see Dad standing in the doorway.

"How would you like to go camping before vacation's over?" he asked.

I knew he was trying to make up for the glacier, but still, camping with Dad sounded okay.

"You can invite Elizabeth and Pamela, too, if you like," he said.

"All *right*!"

"It's a date then. We'll pick a weekend sometime soon," he told me.

I went straight to the phone to call Elizabeth, but it rang just as I got there. It was Pamela. Before I could even tell her about camping, she said, "Alice, that old boyfriend of yours is a creep."

"What did he do?" I asked weakly.

"We met at Wendy's, and things were going great, but then we walked around the mall and he kept looking at his watch. At five minutes to three he said he was meeting a girl at the Orange Bowl."

I gulped.

"Can you *imagine*?"

I imagined, all right.

"And do you know what else he told me? That I'd look great with long hair." And suddenly Pamela burst into tears. The last time I'd seen her crying over her hair was the day in the beauty parlor when they were cutting it off, so I figured she needed another good cry.

"He's not worth it, Pamela," I said. "I've seen you with long and short hair both, and I like it better short."

Then I told her how she and Elizabeth were going camping with Dad and me, and after that we had something else to talk about, so things were okay.

I called Elizabeth.

"Donald Sheavers is a dip," she said.

"I know," I told her.

"We had a shake at the Orange Bowl, and you know what he said? He said I'd look better in short hair."

Maybe Donald was going into the beauty business.

"He's a jerk," I agreed. "Listen, Elizabeth, do you want to go camping?" And I told her all about it.

The next person who called, of course, was Donald Sheavers. "You've got some really weird girlfriends, Alice," he said.

"That's okay, Donald, they loved you, too," I told him. And he actually thought it was a compliment.

But something was really bothering me, and it wasn't Donald Sheavers. Pamela and Elizabeth both were taking chances. Pamela didn't surprise me. *Nothing* Pamela ever does surprises me. But Elizabeth had done two things now that were really hard for her, I knew. Somehow she'd just gritted her teeth and got up the courage and done them.

Yet no matter how much I wanted the kids to like me, to be a part of the gang, I couldn't even imagine myself going in water over my head. The very thought made me break out in a cold sweat, my heart pound. I'd just have to be creative, that's all, and think up new excuses, I told myself. I'd have to make sure I was always near Mark's house, so if the guys started horsing around, I could run inside. I mean, if I was diabetic, I'd always have to be careful of what I ate, wouldn't I? So why couldn't I look at this as sort of a health problem, too, and make sure I never got near the deep end?

I didn't have to make up an excuse not to go over to the Stedmeisters' pool on Saturday, because I work at Dad's music store for three hours on Saturdays. Actually, my boss is Janice Sherman, the assistant manager, who's in charge of sheet music, and I also do whatever Loretta Jenkins needs doing. Loretta runs the Gift Shoppe.

I helped record a music shipment. Janice, in a brown linen dress, with her glasses hanging on a chain around her neck, was efficiently answering the phone and filing a pile of letters in her lap at the same time. Janice, who once had a crush on my father and probably still does, looked as though she was never afraid of anything in her whole life, and suddenly I found myself saying, "Janice, how do you get over being afraid of something?"

She'd just hung up the phone and put her glasses back on. Now she studied me over the top of the frames.

"It depends. Anything in particular?"

"Oh, things that you shouldn't be afraid of, mostly, but you are."

For a long time it seemed that Janice Sherman honestly couldn't think of a thing. Maybe she'd gone her whole life without being afraid once.

Finally she told me, "The one thing I was afraid of when

I was young was public speaking, but then someone told me it's the *audience* that's frightened. They're afraid you're going to speak too long, or be boring, or that they won't understand you. It's your job to make them feel at ease. When I looked at it *that* way–that I was standing up before a roomful of people who were afraid of *me*–I just wasn't scared anymore. It was the strangest thing."

I thought about that as I checked in the rest of the music. It just didn't seem to apply, somehow. Nothing could convince me that the water in Mark Stedmeister's swimming pool was as afraid of me as I was of it. Maybe it was a good thing Janice never married and had a daughter, because I doubted she would be any help to one at all.

The weird thing was, when I asked Loretta Jenkins the same question, she said the only way to overcome your fear of something was practice, practice, practice–that when she was in junior high she had this fear of kissing, so she simply told herself to practice, practice, practice and never dreamed how much fun it would be once she caught on.

"How can you do a lot of something you can't even get up your nerve to do for the very first time?" I asked.

"Just close your eyes and let it happen," she said.

Loretta wasn't much help either.

Aunt Sally called that evening.

"How are things, Alice? Summer's almost over, you know. I can't believe you'll soon be starting eighth grade."

"Me either," I told her.

"How's Lester?"

"Still dating Marilyn Rawley and seeing Crystal Harkins on the side," I said.

"He likes to live dangerously. And your dad?"

"Fine. He said he had a good time in Michigan."

"Michigan? He went to Michigan without stopping to see us?"

"Well, Chicago's not exactly on the way, Aunt Sally," I told her. "He and Miss Summers had a direct flight."

I knew immediately, by the silence at the other end, that I had not only failed to tell her that Dad was going to the music conference at all, but I had not mentioned that he was traveling "in the company of a woman," as Aunt Sally would have put it.

"Your English teacher?" she asked. "What does she know about music?"

"She sings. She even took a class in flamenco dancing."

Now I knew I'd really done it. Aunt Sally, who has never met Miss Summers, would forever after imagine her as a flamenco dancer with a rose between her teeth.

"So your father has a traveling companion," she said finally.

"They had separate rooms," I told her.

"I didn't ask about sleeping arrangements," said Aunt Sally. More silence. Then, "On the same floor?"

"No, they were in a dormitory. Men on one floor, women another."

Aunt Sally sighed. "Tell me about your teacher, Alice.

What's she like?"

Why did I feel that no matter what I told her about Miss Summers, my teacher would never be good enough for my dad in Aunt Sally's eyes? Never be the kind of woman my mom was? I knew for a fact that whatever I said would be wasted on Aunt Sally, so I just said the first thing that came into my head.

"She wears a black lace slip with a slit up the side."

"Other than that," said Aunt Sally.

"When she comes over, she leans against the piano and sings while Dad plays," I added.

"Anything else?" Aunt Sally asked plaintively.

It was amazing the things that stuck in my mind. "She doesn't make her bed," I said, remembering the time Miss Summers had invited me to her home to make Dad's birthday cake. "I've been in her house, and I know."

A sigh came over the line.

"And she leaves her clothes lying around." That was true, but it was just a pair of slippers here, a sweater there.

"Friends of mine have seen her and Dad holding hands at a restaurant," I went on, desperate for anything. "That's about all I can think of, except that she's a really great teacher."

"It sounds pretty serious to me, Alice," Aunt Sally said at last. "What do you think?"

"I *hope* so! She's really nice."

"Well," said Aunt Sally. "If she's a great teacher, I guess it's all right if she doesn't make her bed, isn't it?"

4

ARMPITS

I knew I couldn't hold off forever, and when Pamela called on Sunday and said the gang was gathering at Mark's pool that afternoon, I put on my bathing suit like a girl facing her execution and went across the street to walk with Elizabeth.

Mrs. Price was sitting out on the front porch fanning herself. She was beginning to look really huge, and I wondered what it would feel like to carry a baby around in your abdomen so that every time you leaned forward you knew you were squishing it just a little.

I guess one of the things that scares me most when I think of having a baby is morning sickness. Throwing up is my least favorite thing to do. The thought of saying "Good morning" to my husband, then *brrraaaghack!* and spilling my cookies is really scary.

"How are you feeling?" I asked Mrs. Price.

She covered her mouth with one hand and waved me on with the other. "Don't ask," she mumbled.

Elizabeth and Pamela and I always put on shorts and Tshirts over our bathing suits and take them off when we get to Mark's. This is the part that Elizabeth hates.

"It's like a striptease!" she said as we walked over.

"Practice, practice, practice," I said, quoting Loretta Jenkins. "You'll have to do it some day in front of your husband, Elizabeth, so just look at this as practice."

Elizabeth stared straight ahead.

"Alice, would you still be my friend . . . twenty years from now, I mean . . . if I never got married?"

"Of course! What does getting married have to do with it?"

"But then you and Pamela would have stuff to talk about, and I'd feel left out, and . . ."

"Why are you trying to figure out your whole life right now?" I asked. "Maybe in twenty years you'll be married and I won't."

Elizabeth shook her head. "I just don't think I can go through with it. The sex part."

"We're all a little scared of that, Elizabeth."

"It wasn't . . . wasn't so bad when I thought it was just . . . intercourse!"

She had actually said that word. I knew how hard it was for her.

"But . . . after the other night . . . when I found out about foreplay and everything . . . Oh, Alice, I just can't do that."

"Nobody's asking you to do that, Elizabeth! That's a long time off with a man you really love that you haven't even met yet." Elizabeth is brave and Elizabeth is honest, but she is also a little nuts.

"Do you think it could be in the marriage contract—there won't be any foreplay?"

"I suppose you can put in anything you want. You can even make him promise never to open the door while you're in the bathroom," I joked.

Elizabeth brightened up. "Really?" She actually seemed to be walking a little livelier, as though maybe she could live through eighth grade after all. There are times I *know* Elizabeth was dropped on her head as a baby.

Pamela was already at the pool this time, sitting at the end of the diving board, legs dangling over the edge.

Why is it that what seems so easy for one person is so hard for another? It didn't bother me at all to unzip my shorts and step out in my bathing suit, yet it was desperately difficult for Elizabeth. But I couldn't climb up on the diving board and sit dangling my legs over the deep end anymore than I could sing in public; Pamela did it without a second thought.

Most of the kids I hung around with were there—Mark, of course, who's been going with Pamela since sixth grade; Brian, the one who put gum in Pamela's hair; Karen and Jill, who had started an earring club once; and a few other kids from school.

"Hey, Alice, when will Patrick be back?" Brian yelled just before he did a "cannonball."

"End of the month," I said, down by the three-foot marker,

splashing water up over my freckled legs. Nobody would ever mistake mine for alabaster.

I tried not to look at Pamela while she was getting ready to do a back flip. But my eyes kept watching as she got her balance on the edge of the board, then propelled herself backward, turning a somersault in the air, and stretching out just in time to dive into the water, bob back up again, and swim around the deep end.

What was I afraid would happen to me if I tried a simple jump? I wondered. I tried to imagine myself going up the ladder to the diving board. Imagined myself walking out to the end and then jumping off. Holding my nose and just jumping right off, hitting the water feet first, going down, down, down, the way Pamela did, and then . . . never to be seen again.

Getting a lungful of water. Passing out. Being hauled out by Mark Stedmeister's father and taken to the morgue.

No matter how many times I watched Pamela dive to the bottom and come up again, I knew beyond a doubt that I would be the person who sank like a rock. I knew that as soon as I realized the water was over my head, I would panic, tense, stiffen, and sink.

Every time I go over to Mark Stedmeister's, I have an excuse ready, and this time he provided it for me, because we'd only been at the pool an hour when Mark set up the badminton set between the trees, and for the rest of the afternoon I was in safe territory. But how long before my luck ran out?

When we took a break and sprawled out on the grass, Jill

said, "You know what we are? The Swim Kids."

"What?" asked Mark.

"Swim Kids . . . Pool Group . . . Water Wonders. Something like that," Jill went on. "You know all those cliques there were in eighth grade last year. The Takoma Five. The Music Bunch. The Baseball Nuts. The Photography Freaks. We've been getting together at Mark's pool for a long time now, and we could be known as the Pool Group or something."

I could feel my muscles tense.

The boys thought it was sort of corny, but I could tell that the girls liked the idea right off.

"I mean, when the other kids want to talk about us, they wouldn't have to recite all our names; they'll just say the 'Pool Group,' and everyone will know who they mean," Jill went on.

"Why would they want to talk about us?" asked Brian.

"They might want to mention the gorgeous girls and the handsome studs," said Mark.

Everyone laughed, including me. It's amazing how you can set your face on automatic. Your lips stretch and your eyes crinkle and you make little chuckling noises in your throat all the while you're feeling sicker and sicker inside. I didn't belong there anymore than I belonged on stage at the Metropolitan Opera. I was as phony as a three-dollar bill. At least Elizabeth had the courage to talk about the things that bothered her. I was too afraid to even say I was scared.

Marilyn Rawley was there when I got home. She was sitting on the couch with her guitar, and Lester was sitting on the piano bench with his. They were playing and singing some old Simon and Garfunkel songs. I got a Pepsi and listened from the doorway of the living room, dripping water from my swimsuit onto the floor.

Marilyn's a small girl with long straight brown hair. She usually wears either jeans or long cotton dresses, the kind of girl you see on the front of a J. Crew catalog. If Lester married Marilyn, I'll bet they'd live in a cabin out in the woods, and all their kids would go barefoot.

She smiled at me when the song was over.

"You look cool," she said.

"I've been over at a friend's pool," I told her.

"Best place to be," said Marilyn.

Lester went up to the bathroom, and I was just getting up my nerve to ask Marilyn if she'd ever been afraid of deep water when she said, "Sometime I'd like to go scuba diving. It's one thing I've always wanted to do that I never got the chance."

I decided that Marilyn wasn't the one to talk to, either.

When we were having dinner that night, I got an idea. I was thinking about the girl who brought a note to school last year because she had a heart condition and couldn't take gym. What if I carried a card with me at all times, signed by Dad, saying that I'm allergic to chlorine and can't ever get water up my nose?

"How do you know when you're allergic to something?" I asked.

"You break out in hives, your eyes roll back, and your body goes into spasms," said Lester.

Dad gave him a look. "You usually break out in a rash, Al. Why? What do you think you're allergic to?"

"Chlorine."

"How so?"

"Oh, I sort of itch after I've been in Mark's swimming pool," I said.

"Sounds more like a sun sensitivity to me," said Dad. "Maybe we ought to have the doctor look you over."

"Not!" I said. "Why can't you just give me a note saying I can't get water up my nose?"

"Why should I give you a note?" said Dad. "If you don't want water up your nose, don't put it there."

"Al, if you were allergic to chlorine, you'd start itching every time you took a drink of water," said Lester.

They had me there.

Monday I stayed home from the pool, but the day wasn't a total loss because that night Dad took me to Sears after we ate, and I picked out a bedroom set. My first thought was that since I was probably soon to be an ex-member of the Pool Group, plus I probably wouldn't have another friend for the rest of my natural life, all I needed was a hammock suspended from the ceiling and wicker baskets for clothes. I could fill the rest of the space with plants, so that when I went to my room it would be like going on safari. No one would be able to find me, and I'd never have to clean any-thing—just water it.

Dad suggested I choose a double bed, so if we ever had a houseful of company there would be more sleeping space. I got a double bed with a long low dresser and chest of drawers, and drapes and a bedspread with a jungle motif—lions and leopards mingled with exotic plants. And because I'd chosen one of the least expensive sets, Dad said I really could have a large rubber plant in one corner. He even bought me a pillow shaped like a koala for the bed. The stuff was delivered two days later, and when everything was set up, it looked like the kind of exotic bedroom where Scheherazade would have entertained her sultan.

I had to invite Elizabeth and Pamela for a sleep-over, of course, and they loved the room. They said I had good taste, but you know what's weird? When you're worried about the one big thing that's wrong with you, nothing else seems to matter. I wasn't Alice of the Good Taste or Alice with a Good Sense of Rhythm, but Alice the Girl Who Can't Go in Water Over Her Head. Only nobody knew it, which made it even worse.

"Look, Alice, there's still sawdust in the drawers," Elizabeth said. She helped me sort my underclothes and match my panties and socks so that everything was color coordinated. Only Elizabeth would think of that.

What I liked most about the double bed was that we could all stretch out on it at the same time and talk, and we'd brought Dad's old army cot up from the basement to put alongside it, so we could even roll off onto that.

We were lying there talking about school and earrings and boys and cramps when I noticed two things: Elizabeth seemed quieter than usual, and somebody smelled.

It was the kind of sweaty odor you smell when you've run two blocks in hot weather to catch the bus. I hoped it wasn't me. The next time I stretched and put my arms up over my head, I turned my nose to one side and sniffed an armpit. Then the other.

Nope. Not me. I could still smell the roll-on I'd used that morning. Musk, I think.

Seemed to me that I'd been noticing that sweaty smell a lot lately, and I wondered which of the two hadn't tried deodorant yet—Pamela or Elizabeth. I hadn't been using one myself for very long, and probably wouldn't be doing it yet, except that one day when I was on my way to the shower, Lester poked his head out of his room and said, "Hey, Al! Present! Catch!" and tossed me a Lady Mennen. I guess if you stink and your brother has to tell you about it, that's as kind a way as any.

Pamela was talking about who had been most popular at school in seventh grade and who hadn't, and what subjects she was going to like most in eighth and which she was going to hate. At some point I got up to get Patrick's postcard from Canada to show them, and when I crawled back onto the bed, I noticed that Elizabeth was lying on her side, a tear rolling down the side of her nose.

"Elizabeth," I said, "what's wrong?"

Pamela stopped talking and looked over. "What's the matter?"

Elizabeth shook her head and quickly wiped the tear. "Nothing." Maybe it was Elizabeth who smelled! Maybe she just realized who it was and was dying of embarrassment.

"Come on, Elizabeth, what *is* it?" I asked. "People don't just cry for nothing."

The tears came even faster. Elizabeth sat up and blew her nose. "I wish I hadn't read you what I did from *Arabian Nights*," she said.

I stared.

"That was a week ago!" I told her. "You weren't crying then."

"Well, I've been thinking about it a lot lately, and I just feel bad, that's all."

"Why?" asked Pamela. "If your parents had it on their bookshelf, then why couldn't you read it?"

"Because it was *their* book, and I didn't ask."

I guess different families do things differently. It would never occur to me to ask Dad or Lester if I could read a book I found in our house, just as I wouldn't feel I had to ask if I found something to eat in the fridge. I'd figure that as a member of the family, I was entitled to it.

"Well, you can quit crying because I've forgotten most of what you read to us," said Pamela, going over to the mirror, wetting one finger with her tongue, and running the finger along her eyebrows to make them darker.

Elizabeth looked hopeful. "Have you forgotten it, Alice?"

Since this was a moral problem of deciding right from wrong, it just didn't seem the place to lie.

"No," I said. I didn't tell Elizabeth, but just that morning I had been thinking about Nubian lasciviousness, wondering what the heck it was. In fact, all it takes is somebody telling me to forget something, and I'll remember it the rest of my life.

"See?" said Elizabeth, clouding up again. "That's two things I've got to confess."

"What do you mean?"

"I not only read the book without asking permission, but I read it to *you* guys, and tainted you, too."

Tainted?

"Listen, Elizabeth. I forgive you, if that makes you feel any better," I told her. "You don't have to confess because of me."

"I'm glad to know that, Alice." Elizabeth blew her nose again. "But I have to know that God forgives me. So the next time I go to confession, I'm going to tell the priest."

"Whatever," said Pamela, over by the mirror.

I'd promised the girls we could have midnight waffles, which is a special treat at our house. It's when you get so hungry in the middle of the night you can't stand it, so you go downstairs and make any kind of waffles you like–orange pecan, chocolate chip, cinnamon mocha. . . . We decided not to wait until midnight, so we started the waffles around eleven, and the aroma filled the house. Lester ate one with us when he came home from Marilyn Rawley's, and Dad even came down in his robe after he'd gone to bed, and asked for a chocolate chip and orange peel waffle, which is my favorite.

It was when Pamela reached across the table to give Dad his waffle that I realized it was Pamela's armpits that smelled. It was hard to believe, because she's so careful about her face and her fingernails and everything. But there was no mistaking it. Pamela's armpits smelled.

"This is delicious, girls," Dad told us, and Lester put a dollar on the table for a tip.

I let Elizabeth and Pamela have my new double bed, and crawled onto the army cot next to Elizabeth's side. After the lights went out, though, I could her hear reciting her rosary, so I knew that despite the waffle break, she was still worried about *Arabian Nights*. When she stopped finally and grew quiet, I could hear Pamela's deep breathing on the other side of her, and decided to take Elizabeth's mind off confession.

"Elizabeth," I whispered.

"What?"

"I want to ask your advice about a little problem."

She rolled over so that her face was looking down at me in the darkness.

"Pamela doesn't use a deodorant."

"I know."

"What do you think we should do?"

"What *can* we do? Give her a bath? I don't think we can do anything, Alice. Do *I* smell?"

"Huh uh."

"Well if I did, I'd want you to tell me. I mean, what if a boy mentions it to her sometime? She'll say we weren't really her friends or we would have told her."

"You're probably right."

"Are you *sure* I don't smell?" she asked.

"You don't."

"My feet?"

"No."

"Positive? Maybe you should smell them."

"I don't have to smell your feet, Elizabeth."

"My breath?"

"No. Really."

"I knew a girl once who had smelly hair," Elizabeth went on. "Are you sure my hair doesn't smell?" She leaned over the side of the bed and dropped her hair right in my face. It just smelled like hair, that's all.

"Your hair is beautiful, and it doesn't stink," I told her. "Now what are we going to do about Pamela? Maybe we could give her a whole set for her birthday–deodorant, bath salts, talcum, the works."

"Her birthday's already passed, Alice."

"That's true." We thought some more.

"Maybe we could put it in her mailbox with a note saying, 'From a friend'," Elizabeth suggested.

"She'd *know*," I said.

We must have fallen asleep thinking about it, because suddenly it was morning. I was taking a shower when I got an idea. When I went back in the bedroom, wrapped in a towel, I had two deodorant sticks with me. One was musk and one was floral bouquet.

"What do you like best, Pamela?" I said. "Musk or floral bouquet? I can't make up my mind."

Pamela was reading a movie magazine she'd brought with her. She took a sniff of each. "Musk, I guess," she said, and went on reading.

I stood right there, putting it on in front of her just so she could see how it was done, but she didn't even look at me.

"What scent do *you* wear?" I asked.

"I don't wear any at all. I don't need it," Pamela said, eyes on her magazine.

Elizabeth looked at me. I looked at Elizabeth.

"That's what *I* thought until Lester gave me one as a present. Then I got the message," I said.

Pamela put down her magazine. She looked from me to Elizabeth. "Are you guys trying to tell me something?"

"We both use deodorant, Pamela," Elizabeth said. "I wouldn't leave the house without it."

Oh, boy. This was it. The moment of truth. Now Pamela would die of embarrassment and she wouldn't talk to us for a month and . . .

Pamela took the stick out of my hand and opened the top. She held up one arm and smeared some in her armpit.

Then the other arm. Then she handed the deodorant back to me and went on reading her magazine. Isn't it weird the way we worry sometimes about things we didn't have to worry about at all?

But Elizabeth was still troubled about *Arabian Nights*, and I was still worried about deep water. Pamela's mother came by to take her to the mall, so Elizabeth was the last to leave. I walked her to the front door.

"When you're really worried about something, Elizabeth, what do you do? Other than confession, I mean?"

"Pray about it," Elizabeth said.

I went back up in my room and sat on my new bed. Then I put my hands in my lap and closed my eyes and tried hard to concentrate on the picture of Jesus at the front of our family Bible.

Dear Jesus Christ, I prayed. *Help me learn to jump off the diving board into deep water.*

I was afraid that might not do it, so I tried again: *Dear Jesus, if I ever fall in the deep end, don't let me drown.*

To be honest, I wasn't entirely sure what a real prayer sounded like, so I tried to think what Elizabeth would say if she were doing the praying: *Dear Jesus, if I ever drown, take me to heaven. Amen.*

The thing is, when I was asking Elizabeth's advice about Pamela the night before, why didn't I ask her for advice about myself? Why did I go on letting chance after chance slip by for confiding in my two closest friends?

Because everyone would be after me then to *do* something about my fear, and I just couldn't. It was the scariest thing in the world to me, and things that are *that* scary, you keep to yourself.

I don't know what connection God has to Aunt Sally, but I think it's very, very odd that that same night, Aunt Sally called again. Of course, she didn't exactly call to talk about my fear of deep water, because she didn't even know about it. What she called to find out, actually, after she'd beat around the bush a little, was whether my English teacher was Catholic, Protestant, or something else.

"I don't know," I told her. "She sang in the *Messiah* sing-along last Christmas, but maybe she just likes to sing."

"Oh," said Aunt Sally. "Well, what have *you* been up to, Alice?"

"I've been going swimming a lot," I told her. I even lie to Aunt Sally. I shouldn't have said swimming, I should have said pool sitting.

"In the public pool?"

"No, actually it's a pool belonging to a friend."

"No lifeguard?" asked Aunt Sally.

"No. The kids just keep an eye on each other, that's all."

"Are the parents even there?"

"Mark's mom is there, but she stays inside mostly."

"Alice, this is a very dangerous situation," Aunt Sally said. "One of you could be drowning and the others not even know it."

My thoughts exactly. Maybe God was warning me through his prophet Sally.

"Now listen," said Aunt Sally. "Here's what my grandmother used to tell me, and I think you'll find it useful. You'll increase your chances of staying alive 100 percent if you just paint a wine cork red, put it on a string, and wear it around your neck every time you go in the water. Then, if you are ever floating unconscious six inches below the surface, the cork will bob around on top and someone will notice."

I tried to imagine going to Mark Stedmeister's with a wine cork around my neck. I tried to imagine the kids all eating pizza beside the pool, glancing out over the water, seeing the cork, and saying, "Oh, look! There's Alice. Do you think we should pull her out?"

What I imagined instead was somebody getting his arm tangled up in the string and accidentally strangling me under the water.

"Thanks, Aunt Sally," I told her. "I'll look for a cork as soon as I hang up."

I sat staring at the telephone. I felt worse than I had before. Which would I rather do, wear a cork around my neck or drown? Which would I rather do? Die of drowning or die of embarrassment?

Four weeks of vacation left, and I wasn't any closer to solving my problem than I was before. I knew one thing, though. If I ever left the Pool Group, I'd still have Patrick. Patrick is so mature for his age that he doesn't care much what the other kids do. If there was ever a guy who makes his own rules, it's Patrick.

So what if the other kids got together around Mark's pool every summer all the way through high school? So what if they became known in eighth grade as the Pool Group, or the Swim Kids, and I wasn't a part of it? Patrick and I would find things to do together. Maybe we'd become known as the Beautiful Couple and everyone would envy us! And suddenly, four weeks before school began, things didn't look so bad after all.

5

SPIES

*D*ad said he could take us camping the following Saturday, and that Miss Summers was going with us. When I told Elizabeth and Pamela, all they could talk about was where she was going to sleep.

Everyone talks about sleep when they mean sex. "Do you think he's sleeping with her?" people say, when they *really* mean, "Are they having intercourse?"

"You know, Dad," I said at dinner that night, "a lot of people are really very curious about you and Miss Summers. If you'd just come right out and say whether or not you're having sex with her, then people could think about other things."

"Other people, meaning you," said Dad.

"I mean Pamela and Elizabeth and . . . everybody!"

"Then there are a lot of people worrying about something that isn't their business in the least," said Dad. "There are, Al, believe it or not, many things in this world that are just as important, if not more so, than sex."

"There are?" asked Lester.

"Does anyone ask if we're having interesting conversations?" Dad continued. "Why is it that the only thing that interests other people is whether or not we're having sex?"

"Hey, Dad, don't knock it," said Lester.

I thought about Dad's question, though. "I guess it's because sex is one of the few things you do in private, so that's what everyone is curious about. And maybe they think that if two people are having sex, they've already *had* interesting conversations."

"Wrong!" said Lester. "I know guys who sleep with girls and don't even know their last names."

"That's what I'm talking about," said Dad.

"Well, just tell me where Miss Summers is going to sleep on this camping trip, and then I won't ask anything else," I told him.

"In a tent all by herself," Dad declared. "Satisfied?"

I nodded. I kept thinking that if Dad would just hurry up and propose, they could sleep in the same tent. Then I could go to sleep out under the stars knowing that I finally had a mom.

On Saturday, Dad and I both took the day off work at the Melody Inn. Elizabeth came over with her sleeping bag, Dad drove us to Pamela's, and then we all went to Saul Road in Bethesda, and the tiny little house where Miss Summers lives.

With some people, everything about them seems

perfect. It seemed perfect that Sylvia Summers should live in a tiny house surrounded by trees and flowers, that her last name should be Summers, that she should have blue eyes and brown hair, and that she should teach English.

All three of us watched breathlessly as Dad went up to the door and waited, and Miss Summers came out in a pair of jeans and sneakers, a blue and white shirt tied in front at the waist.

"Hi, girls," she said, as she helped put her stuff in the trunk. "Guess I'm the official den mother or something, huh?"

"Hello, Miss Summers," said Elizabeth, as though she were still in class.

It wasn't until we were on Route 270, heading toward Sugarloaf Mountain, that we all began to relax. Dad readjusted the radio so that the music played mostly in the back seat, and tuned it to our favorite station. But Pamela, Elizabeth, and I sat watching every move Dad or Miss Summers made, listening to every word. We'd be chattering away and then Dad would turn to Miss Summers and say something, and we'd stop talking in midsentence. Or Miss Summers would lean her head back against the seat, her hair falling over the edge, and we'd fix our eyes on it, noticing how shiny it looked.

Pamela found a couple gray hairs, and silently pointed them out to me, and then we started guessing all over again how old we thought she was.

Thirty-eight, Elizabeth wrote on a piece of paper. Pamela

shook her head and crossed it out. *Forty-three,* she corrected.

I really didn't care if her hair was all white. White hair and blue eyes, with a long white wedding gown and a bouquet of tiny blue and white flowers.

What I had imagined was that we would be camping beside a crystal lake, and somehow I would get up the nerve to swim out to a raft beside Miss Summers. I would want to please my teacher so much that I would get up my nerve and suddenly, miraculously, overcome my fear of deep water.

But when we turned off 270 and got where we were going, there wasn't any lake at all. Dad parked out in a meadow near the base of Sugarloaf Mountain, and there was just a shallow little stream we could have crawled through on our hands and knees.

Miss Summers didn't seem to mind at all. As we got out of the car, she said, "This is a first for me. I've never been camping in my life."

Dad looked surprised. "Never?"

"Unless you count sleeping in a tent in the backyard with my sister."

"Sorry, doesn't count." Dad smiled. And then, "Okay, all hands on deck. You girls stick around long enough to get the tents up, and then you can explore."

Once we all had something to do, we didn't gawk at Miss Summers the way we had. We felt around on the ground until we found a spot without any rocks or roots in it. We helped Dad set up his tent, Dad helped Miss

Summers put up hers, and by that time we could put up ours by ourselves.

"I've brought my field glasses," Miss Summers said, lifting the hair up off the back of her neck to cool. "Would you believe I've seen most of the birds that are found in the mid-Atlantic states, but I've yet to see a Baltimore oriole?"

"Well, I suppose you might have to go to Baltimore for that, but let's give it a try," Dad told her. "Anybody want to take a hike up Sugarloaf?"

I felt Pamela nudge me. "No," I said. "We're going to walk along the creek."

It was after they disappeared through the trees that Pamela said, "You want to follow them? I'll bet they're going to make love."

"Pamela!" Elizabeth frowned. She sure didn't want any more on her conscience.

"I only said the obvious," Pamela declared. "Didn't you see the tender way he looked at her when she lifted up her hair like that, and her breasts sort of rose? They'll find some grassy spot halfway up the trail and make love."

Elizabeth was staring in spite of herself. "Outdoors?"

"Of *course!*" said Pamela. "Under the trees, beside the ocean, on the sand, in the water . . ."

In the water? I'm sure I looked as shocked as Elizabeth did. Did this mean that when I got older I had to worry not only about keeping my head above water, but knowing how to make love at the same time? The possibility of a drowning death was looking more certain all the time.

"Well, I don't want to hear about it," said Elizabeth, and she meant it. "Come on. Let's go to the creek."

We all traipsed down the hill to look for crawdads, and forgot about things we didn't have to worry about then. It was just fun to be outdoors. Everything smelled different—fresh and warm when we were walking in the meadow, dank and earthy when we walked along the creek. Our footsteps made crunchy sounds in the weeds, squishy sounds on the bank, and even the breeze felt different on our faces than it did back home.

Every so often we found a place we could cross, and stopped to watch all the stuff swimming around. Elizabeth could name each fish and insect and would have made our seventh-grade science teacher proud. I was mostly concerned about getting to the other side without my foot going in.

By the time we got back, we were starved. Dad and Miss Summers had already started dinner.

"How does grilled chicken and corn on the cob sound?" Miss Summers called when she saw us. "I could use some help shucking the corn."

It sounded wonderful. She held up a bag of corn, and we set to work, while she cut some peppers, onions, and mushrooms into strips, sprinkled them with olive oil, and put them over the coals.

"How come we're the only ones camping out here?" she asked Dad, as the chicken sizzled over the fire.

"Because it's private property. One of my customers

owns the land. He lets the Scouts use it occasionally, so I figured it was good enough for us."

That got me thinking. "So where's the bathroom?" I was surprised Elizabeth hadn't asked yet. She's usually pretty particular about things like that.

"Don't ask," Miss Summers said, and she and Dad both laughed.

Elizabeth froze.

"There's an outhouse of sorts beyond the trees over there," Dad said, "and up there by the fence at the horse pasture, you'll find a faucet for washing up."

Elizabeth never moved.

It was a good dinner, and I could tell that Dad was enjoying it. Both the food, and having Miss Summers sitting there in her jeans, her hair fastened up off the nape of her neck with a comb.

Maybe it was watching Miss Summers eat chicken with her fingers that relaxed us, but by the time she'd got through her corn on the cob, she didn't seem like our teacher any longer—just an older cousin, maybe, or a favorite aunt who was along on a picnic.

Elizabeth hardly said a word throughout the meal, though, and as soon as it was over, she whispered, "Alice, I'm about to burst. Go to the restroom with me?"

"The *restroom*?" I said. Only Elizabeth would call an outhouse a restroom.

Pamela said she'd come, too, so all three of us headed in

the direction where Dad had pointed.

When we got to the outhouse, we found no house at all, just a tiny shelter with a roof and three sides, and a bench with two holes in it over a shallow pit.

Elizabeth stared. "What *is* it?"

"Toilet," I said.

"What's the second hole for?"

"Whoever else has to go."

"No!" Elizabeth cried. "I won't use this thing, Alice. I . . ."

"Elizabeth, shut up," said Pamela. "Just go."

"Don't watch!" Elizabeth whimpered.

We turned our backs to her, but I couldn't help yelling, "There's the farmer, galloping this way on horseback!" and Elizabeth almost fell off the john.

We sat around the campfire that night eating s'mores with Miss Summers. Dad said he'd never seen anything so disgusting in his life as the little graham cracker, marshmallow, Hershey's bar concoctions we were melting over the fire. I guess any girl who has ever been a Girl Scout, seen a Girl Scout, or heard of a Girl Scout knows how to make s'mores.

As usual, though, I was just beginning to enjoy myself when somebody started singing old camp songs. Even though Elizabeth and Pamela both know I can't carry a tune, they forget sometimes. Dad knew right away how I was feeling, because when they started the second song, he put his arm around my shoulder, and as much as I wanted to snuggle up against him, it's not the sort of thing you do in front of your friends. Then I got this brilliant idea.

"Why don't you and Miss Summers sing a duet, Dad?" I said.

"Like what? Are we taking requests?" he asked.

"Well . . . the *Messiah*, maybe?" I suggested.

Dad threw back his head and laughed, and Miss Summers joined in. It had a wonderful rhythm to it, their laughter–Dad's tenor and Miss Summers's alto.

"How about 'Scarborough Fair'?" Miss Summers said. "Only I wish we had a guitar. Ben, can you do the canticle?"

Dad said he thought he could, that he might not know all the words but he'd wing it.

I wouldn't know a canticle from a cuticle, but Miss Summers began, and Dad joined in, and about halfway through the song, I realized that Miss Summers was singing one set of words and Dad was singing another. It was as though they were singing two different songs entirely, but it was beautiful.

When it was over, I could see Dad's hand sort of move along the ground, and his fingers close over Miss Summers's fingers there in the light of the campfire. I yawned and said it was time for bed, and gave Elizabeth and Pamela a look. Was this the night Dad would propose? It was all I could think about after we'd crawled into our tent.

6

𝒯ENT TALK

"𝓑oy, have *they* ever got the hots!" said Pamela as soon as we'd zipped up our tent.

"They don't have the *hots*, Pamela! They're in love with each other," I said. Now *I* was beginning to sound like Elizabeth, but when it's my dad we're talking about, I didn't want the way he feels about Miss Summers to just be "the hots."

"Well, excuse *me*!" said Pamela. "He *doesn't* have the hots for her, then."

That didn't sound quite right either.

"Being in love is probably a whole lot of things," I told her.

We'd no sooner put on our pajamas than all three of us had to go to the toilet, so we crawled out of our tent with a lot of coughing in advance so Dad would know we were coming. He had his arm around Miss Summers there by the fire, but he got up to get us a flashlight, and we set off.

"When we get back, let's go right to sleep, because if I

have to go to the bathroom again before morning, I'll never go alone," Elizabeth said.

I don't think we'd noticed all the hopping kinds of things there were in the field before. Pamela started to step on a stone and discovered it wasn't a stone at all. It was a toad that hopped right at her. She screamed and then we all screamed, and when we got back Dad said it sounded like a massacre over by the outhouse.

He and Miss Summers were still there by the campfire, backs against a log. She had her knees drawn up, arms wrapped around her legs. We told them about the frog, and they laughed.

"If I have to go in the night, may I wake one of you girls to go with me?" Miss Summers asked. I couldn't tell if she was teasing or not.

"I'll go," I said. "Just poke me, and I'll get right up."

I meant it, too. I'd walk right through that field holding the flashlight for her, and I imagined us both sitting down side by side on the two holes of the toilet and her telling me that Dad had proposed.

Do you know what's weird? What's weird is lying in a tent with your two best friends while your father and his girlfriend are smooching out in the dark. I suppose this is the way Dad will feel about me some day. He'll be in bed listening to me come home with a guy, and he'll wonder what we're doing downstairs. What we're talking about.

"What do you suppose men ask women when they go out together?" I said suddenly. "I mean, what do they really want to know about them?"

We lay there thinking about that.

"What does Mark ask you?" Elizabeth said to Pamela.

"If I've ever been to a roller derby. When you were going out with Tom Perona, what did he ask you?" Pamela said in return.

"He used to ask me if his hands were sweaty," Elizabeth said, remembering. "What about Patrick, Alice?"

"He asked which I liked best—Mars or Milky Way."

We were quiet a long while.

"Do you suppose boys are just born that way?" I asked finally.

"It's probably passed down from father to son, something in the genes," said Pamela.

I think we were all amazed, when we stopped talking, how *noisy* it was out here in the field. No horns or traffic, of course, but the insects had started a symphony concert. In the direction of the trees we could hear skitterings and scratchings, scufflings and slitherings. As though there was a whole world that came out after dark.

Elizabeth went to sleep first, then Pamela. I just felt too excited. Like something wonderful was going to happen out there by the campfire—the way you feel on Christmas Eve when you're a little kid, and you think you hear sleigh bells and stuff.

I was thinking about how a lot of life is taking chances. I mean, that's what life *is*, really. Dad had taken a chance that Miss Summers would go on a camp-out with him and a bunch of girls. And after she said she would, he was taking a chance he'd have some time alone with her. And then, when he did, he was probably taking the biggest risk of all and proposing to her.

I guess I went to sleep after all because I remember dreaming that it was morning, and Dad and Miss Summers looked really happy, but they wouldn't tell me anything. And then I realized it was the middle of the night, and I had to go to the toilet. *Why* had I drunk that second glass of lemonade? I could be sleeping peacefully like Pamela, or snoring like Elizabeth, if only I had stuck with one glass.

I rolled around a little, hoping that either Pamela or Elizabeth would wake up and go with me, but neither of them stirred. So finally I crawled out of my sleeping bag and crept outside.

The sky looked alive. I couldn't ever remember, in my whole life, looking up and seeing so many stars. So many *bright* stars. Like the sky is different out here than it is back in Silver Spring.

It was about then I discovered I didn't have the flashlight and didn't know where it was. And I wasn't about to walk through the field by myself in the dark, so I just went off into the weeds, squatted down, and studied the stars.

I made my way back to the glow of the campfire when somebody said, "Can't sleep, Al?"

"Dad!" I whispered.

He was sitting on a log back by the trees, so I went over.

$\mathscr{L}$ETTERS

$\mathscr{T}$here is one big difference between the mail that leaves our house and the mail that comes in. The stamps are different. Whenever the government puts out a stamp honoring a musician or composer, Dad buys about three hundred of them. We had so many Gershwin stamps we had to keep them in a shoebox until we found space in a desk drawer.

When I get mail, which is about five times a year, Dad or Lester puts it on the mantel, and a few days after the camping trip, I came home from the library to find an envelope with no return address.

Patrick, I thought, tearing it open.

From St. Jude, it read. *With love, all things are possible.*

It sure wasn't from Patrick. I kept reading:

This paper has been sent to you for good luck. It has been around the world nine times. You will receive good luck. Send it on to someone you think needs good luck. DO NOT SEND MONEY as fate has no price. This letter must leave your hands within 24 hours.

I felt as though I were holding some kind of holy paper in my hands:

Joe Samuels received $50,000,000 and lost it because he broke the chain. While in Hawaii, Bill Walsh lost his wife after receiving this letter, because he failed to send it on. Mary Phillips received this letter and, not believing, she died!!!

Remember, DO NOT IGNORE THIS! Thank you, St. Jude. You will receive good luck within four days of receiving this letter provided you send it on.

I was afraid that if I didn't mail the letter immediately, I might forget. I wasn't in the mood for taking chances on anything these days, and I sure didn't want to be found dead in my room with this letter still on my dresser. What if I forgot to mail it and then Dad or Lester had a heart attack? The question was, who did I want to have especially good luck? Miss Summers, I decided. I wanted Dad to propose to her again, and this time sound as though he really meant it.

I got an envelope, put the letter inside and sealed it just as the phone rang.

It was Elizabeth.

"I think you ought to go to confession with me," she said.

"What?"

"I'm going to tell the priest about *Arabian Nights*, and I think you and Pamela should come with me, only she's gone to the movies."

"Why should I go with you? *I* wasn't reading that book out loud."

"You *listened,* didn't you? I wouldn't even have brought it over if you and Pamela hadn't badgered me to loosen up."

"Elizabeth, I'm not even Catholic! What am I supposed to say?"

"You can at least come and wait for me outside."

That much I could do for my friend. "If it will make you happy," I said, and mailed the letter to Miss Summers on my way across the street.

I don't think I ever saw Elizabeth in such a serious mood. Nothing I could say would make her laugh, and after a while, I didn't feel so good myself.

"If it *was* a sin, Elizabeth–reading *Arabian Nights* to us–what will happen? I mean, are you excommunicated or something?" I'm not even sure what that means, but it has an X in it, and so does crucifixion, and words with Xs in them mean serious business, sex included, which got Elizabeth into *Arabian Nights* in the first place.

"Of course not," Elizabeth snapped. "It's not a *mortal* sin, after all. It's just so embarrassing to have to tell somebody."

"Tell the priest you just opened the book to Abyssinian sobbings and had to find out what they were talking about," I suggested.

"Cut it out, Alice."

"Well?"

"We never *did* find out what it means. And I didn't just happen to open the book to that page. I read a lot of pages before I found the parts to read aloud. I *chose* them, after all. That makes it all the worse."

I decided that nothing I could say would make Elizabeth feel better, so I just walked along beside her like a faithful dog till we came to the church, and then I sat down and waited on the steps.

"Good luck," I told her.

Every so often somebody came out or someone went in, and I felt like a heathen sitting out there. I felt the most religious–the most awestruck, I suppose–sitting out under the stars with Dad that night near Sugarloaf, thinking how somebody must have planned the universe–drawn up a blueprint, or something. But I suppose religion is like falling in love–different for different people. So I waited patiently for Elizabeth, wishing I had said something more helpful than "good luck."

When she came out fifteen minutes later, she looked a little better but not a lot.

"So are you going to purgatory or what?" I asked as I got up and followed her down the steps. Donald Sheavers used to talk a lot about purgatory, which is somewhere between heaven and hell, he told me.

"No. I guess it wasn't such a stiff sentence after all."

"What do you have to do?"

"Three Hail Marys, one Our Father, and a Glory Be," she said.

I thought a Glory Be was something Aunt Sally would say. "Is that all the priest said?"

"He said it's normal to be curious," Elizabeth replied.

"Well, then!" I said, beginning to like Elizabeth's priest. "That's it? You confess and it's over?"

"No, he says the *real* reason I'm feeling bad about it is because I didn't tell my parents I was taking the book, and he thinks I should confess that to them."

I wasn't so sure about the priest after all. Maybe the reason I didn't like the priest's suggestion was that I was afraid the Prices would put the book away where Elizabeth could never find it, and I never *would* find out what Nubian lasciviousness was.

"Mom will kill me," Elizabeth muttered, and then, her voice trembling, "They'll be so disappointed in me. They don't even know I *know* about things like that."

"Elizabeth, we still don't! The only difference between before and after is that we're even more confused."

But once Elizabeth gets upset, there's no comforting her. I began to wish I'd sent the St. Jude letter to her, because she was going to need all the luck she could get.

When we went inside her house, there was an envelope propped up on the lamp table in the living room. Elizabeth went over and picked it up.

"What is it?" I asked.

She shrugged. "Just mail, I guess." It had her name on it and the same Thomas Jefferson stamp. When she opened it, there was a St. Jude letter just like mine.

"Let me see that envelope," I said, and studied it hard. There was a Takoma Park postmark on the stamp. I should have checked the postmark on mine: Donald Sheavers! *Donald* had sent those letters to us! What a dweeb!

I went right to the phone and called Pamela, but she wasn't home yet.

"Did she get any mail today?" I asked her dad.

"As a matter of fact, she did. A letter, but I don't know who it's from," he said.

"Does it have a Takoma Park postmark?" I asked.

Mr. Jones checked. "Yep. Sure does."

"Thank you very much," I told him.

It's not the kind of thing Donald Sheavers would think up by himself, though. I figured somebody had sent a copy to him, and he decided that all three of us—Pamela, Elizabeth, and I—needed all the luck we could get.

Elizabeth's mother came downstairs from where she'd been resting, and Elizabeth showed the letter to her.

"This is absolute nonsense," she said after she'd read it. "Poor St. Jude, I don't know what he did to deserve this." And she threw the letter in the trash.

Elizabeth didn't think anymore of it, I could tell, because she was already worrying about how she was going to tell her mom about *Arabian Nights*, so I decided it was a good time to go home.

As I crossed the street, however, I was thinking about the envelope and how I could tell it was probably from Donald Sheavers by the postmark. Then I thought about the envelope I had mailed to Miss Summers, and my heart almost stopped beating, because I'd used one of our Gershwin stamps. *Nobody* has Gershwin stamps anymore except us, and she knows it!

As soon as Dad got home from work, I sat down across from him in the living room: "I guess I'd better tell you about the letter," I said. It must have been Confession Day in Silver Spring.

"What letter?"

"I sent a letter to Miss Summers."

"What?" Dad was taking off his shoes, and paused as though he'd been caught in a strobe light.

"From St. Jude."

"Alice, what the devil are you talking about?"

That just made it worse. I told him about the letter and how Miss Summers would know it was from me.

"Why on earth would it even occur to you to send a St. Jude letter to Sylvia?" Dad asked. "Sometimes I just don't understand you at all."

That made two of us. Now I was really in over my head. I felt as though I was going to cry, but that would be too easy. Dad was angry, I could tell.

"I just thought . . . maybe . . . I don't know. . . ."

"You thought what?"

"That maybe, because she . . . probably didn't . . . well, say yes when you proposed. . . ."

"Al, will you please keep out of my business?" He was angry, all right. *Really* angry. "You haven't the slightest notion what's going on between us, yet you get some wild idea in your head and run with it."

Now I was staring. "But . . . but you *did* propose, didn't you?"

"I'm not going to tell you everything that happens between me and Sylvia or any other woman."

I stared. "There's *another* woman?"

"Al!" he bellowed. "You're driving me crazy!"

My voice was so small I could hardly hear it: "Well, I just wish I knew what was going on sometimes."

"So do I! So do I!" said Dad. He threw down his shoe and took off the other. "But get one thing straight, young lady. What goes on between Sylvia and me is strictly between us. You are not to ask her anything, suggest anything, or say anything at all that treats her as something other than a teacher and a friend. Do I make myself clear?"

I felt tears forming in my eyes and blinked. It wasn't because he was scolding me, it was because he was saying in so many words that Miss Summers wasn't anything more to him than that—a friend. In fact, I rarely saw my dad this angry, and this seemed to cancel out the wonderful time we'd had camping.

I sat out on the back steps a long time. Last week had seemed like such a magical time, and now it wasn't magic at all.

Elizabeth called later. "My folks are mad," she said.

"Welcome to the club," I told her.

"Not because I read the book, but because I read it to you and Pamela. Mom says that the book can't leave the house again without her permission."

"Okay, will you ask if I can borrow it then?"

"What?" she cried. "You're crazy, Alice! Honestly, sometimes I just don't understand you at all!"

It was beginning to sound familiar.

I think that of all the times in the past couple of years I'd felt most alone, this was the worst. I needed someone to talk to, and Dad wasn't talking, Lester wasn't home, and I sure didn't want to call Aunt Sally.

I went up to my room and wondered if it was times like this a mom would come in and sit beside you. Put an arm around you and, no matter how you were feeling, say she'd felt like that once when she was your age.

That's how I imagined it would be. Like the mothers on TV, the way they looked at their child when the kid had a little cough. As though this was the most important cough in the world. Would it really be like that, or was this only a fantasy?

At dinner that night, I wanted to find out if Dad was still mad at me. I had to start learning to head off trouble before it started. So when Dad seemed extra quiet, I asked, "Is there any book in the house that you don't want me to read aloud to Pamela and Elizabeth?"

"Not that I can think of offhand," he said. "You starting a book discussion club or something?"

"No. More like . . . uh . . . stories."

"I've got an excellent short-story collection, Al. You're welcome to it."

"Well, not exactly stories," I said, and when Lester gave

me a quizzical look, I said, "More like . . . uh . . . how-to-do-it books."

"How to do *what*?" asked Lester.

"Home decorating? Sewing?" asked Dad.

"Bodies," I told him. "You know. Growing up and everything."

"She wants a sex manual," said Lester.

"*Lester*!" I yelled.

"Al," Dad said, "there isn't any book in this house you can't read, but some are valuable first editions, so I'd prefer you didn't lend them."

"Thanks, Dad," I said, and turned up my nose at Lester.

After dinner I walked slowly along Dad's bookshelves and thumbed through every title that looked as though it had possibilities. I couldn't understand it. The Prices are Catholic, and they had the unexpurgated edition of *Tales from the Arabian Nights*. We don't go to church much, and the closest I could find were love poems by Robert Browning, and *Coming of Age in Samoa*. Was life weird or what?

A second letter came for me the next day. This time I checked the postmark before I opened it. Canada.

Dear Alice,

At least Patrick got the "dear" right.

The way the mail is up here, I suppose I could be

home by the time you get this, but I felt like writing anyway. We're having a great time, but it's still going to be nice to get back and see you.

I felt all warm and mushy inside. It's wonderful to have a boyfriend. To know there's a guy out there who likes you better than any other girl in the whole world. I hope.

I've been thinking about things we could do together in school next year—you know—clubs and stuff. I'd sort of like to work on the school newspaper. Would you like something like that?

The place we're staying here in Banff has an Olympic-size swimming pool, and Dad and I have been having races every day. Mark says there's an eighth-grade swim team that holds meets at the Y. That's something I'd *really* like. How about it? Will you try out with me? We could go to the swim meets together, if we make it.

Save all your kisses for me.

Love, Patrick

$\mathscr{S}$PECTACLE

$\mathscr{I}$ didn't think I could stand it. Patrick was my last hope. Patrick's telling me that if I didn't want to go to the pool anymore, he didn't either. Patrick's saying what was the big deal about being able to swim in water over my head? I had good rhythm, didn't I? Who cared if I couldn't swim? We'd find something else to do. Somewhere else to go. If the other kids wanted to fry themselves out under the August sun, they could, but he and I would take long walks together and talk about important things. . . .

Any other time I would have run to the phone and read his letter aloud to Elizabeth and Pamela. I would have read that last line to myself over and over again–"Save all your kisses for me." And especially, the "love."

Now I knew that my dreams were as phony as the St. Jude letter. As phony as Scheherazade and her thousand and one nights. As Miss July in *Playboy* with her rosy nipples. Patrick was going to try out for the eighth-grade swim team, and if I couldn't go with him, he'd probably find a girl who could.

Elizabeth, Pamela, and I agreed to meet at Mark's the next day, and I walked downstairs like a robot.

"I'm going to Mark's," I said to Dad, standing by his chair while he was working a crossword puzzle.

"Have a good time," he said, not even looking up.

I hesitated, wondering if he was still mad at me.

"Love you," I told him.

"Love you, too," he replied, and smiled at me as he wrote down another word.

If parents knew everything that goes on in their kids' heads, they'd be really surprised, I think. Dad had no idea that I always said "love you" before I went to Mark's pool, so that if that turned out to be the day I sank to the bottom, the last thing I would have said to my father was "love you."

It wasn't exactly the recipe for a fun day, because my fantasy of laughing gaily as the boys tossed me into the deep end was all mixed up with the sound of an ambulance racing down side streets, neighbors gathering, lights flashing, paramedics trying to get me breathing again, and then Dad and Lester coming to the morgue to identify me.

There was a big crowd this time. I guess we all sensed there wasn't much left of summer, and everyone wanted to party, party, party. Jill and Karen were there, some boys I didn't even know, even Tom Perona, Elizabeth's old flame from sixth grade. He goes to St. John's. He broke up with Elizabeth because she wouldn't let him kiss her, and I could tell by the way he was looking at her this time that he wondered if she'd changed any. I knew that all it would take for him to get interested in her again was to find out she had smuggled *Arabian Nights* to a sleep-over and read some of the juicy parts out loud.

I tried to be cheerful for my friends' sakes.

"Elizabeth," I said, when we were lying on our stomachs around the shallow end. "You're all forgiven for taking *Arabian Nights* to Pamela's house, aren't you? I mean, the priest forgives you and your folks forgive you and God forgives you, right?"

"I think so," she said.

"Then would it really mess things up if I just casually mentioned to Tom Perona that you were reading stories from that book?"

Elizabeth looked shocked. "Alice! I sinned, and you're going to go around telling everyone about it?"

"But it's only a statement of fact, right?"

"Yes, but . . ."

"Is it a sin to state a fact?"

"No, but . . ."

"If *I* feel guilty, I'll confess to my father," I promised. "Just say I can do it, Elizabeth."

"Well, I can't control what *you* do," she said, and laid her head back down again. That was a yes if I ever heard one.

I walked over to the side where Tom had just climbed out and was shaking water out of one ear.

"Hi, Tom. Haven't seen you for a while," I said.

"How ya doin'?" He thumped one side of his head.

"Elizabeth looks great, doesn't she?" I commented. Real subtle, that's me.

"She *always* looked great," said Tom, and went on pounding his head.

"Have you talked to her lately? She's really changed," I told him.

Tom glanced in Elizabeth's direction. She was starting to get that S curve that women get when they lie on their stomachs at the beach.

"Different how?" Tom asked.

I shrugged and gave a little laugh. "Oh, just more fun. Not so stiff."

"Yeah?" said Tom.

"She's really crazy, sometimes. We had a sleep-over a couple weeks ago, and you know what she smuggled along?"

"What?" asked Tom, looking interested.

"*Tales from the Arabian Nights.*"

He stared at me blankly. "What's that?"

I forgot that St. John's would be the last school in the world to have that book on its shelf.

"Well, they're pretty racy stories. She was reading them out loud to Pamela and me."

"No kidding?" Tom grinned and looked over at Elizabeth again. Elizabeth was turned the other way.

I spread my towel out on a deck chair, way back from the pool, so that Tom and Elizabeth could get acquainted all over again. The next time I looked that way, I saw Tom

flipping his towel at Elizabeth's bare legs, and she was draw-
ing up her feet and squealing.

I closed my eyes to the sun and tried to think when
Patrick was coming back—what day he'd told me. I was
remembering the way he had kissed me when he walked me
home on his birthday—a really nice kiss, not that quick wet
peck on the lips he'd done back in sixth grade. I had to tell
someone about my fear of deep water, and I decided I'd start
with Patrick. I had worried all this time about what Dad
would do if I told him, or what Elizabeth and Pamela would
do—whether they'd tell the other kids. The person I was
most worried about, though, was Patrick, so I'd tell him as
soon as he got back and get it over with.

My mistake was that I was thinking about Patrick when I
should have been paying attention to what was going on
around me. Because suddenly it seemed to get very quiet,
and I had barely opened one eye when I heard a bunch of
guys yell, "Get Alice!"

Then they were all around me, trying to grab my arms
and legs and I was kicking with every ounce of strength I
had.

I screamed. My fingers closed around the vinyl slats of
the deck chair, and I hung on as though I were being pushed
off the edge of a cliff.

"Get her hands!" someone yelled.

I kicked even harder, but someone had my left foot now.
The boys were tumbling around all over me, trying to get my
feet and hands, and the deck chair collapsed beneath us.

There was this incredible tangle of boys and arms and legs and vinyl slats, and I was screaming, and the next thing I knew I was crying. Big gulping sobs.

As suddenly as it had all begun, the wrestling stopped. I was lying in a heap on the deck chair, and the boys were just standing there awkwardly, staring at me.

I would have been glad to faint right then and wake up in a hospital. Instead, the boys just sort of slunk away. They didn't know how to handle it.

Pamela crouched down beside me, helping me get untangled from the chair.

"What's wrong?" she whispered.

"I panicked."

"Why?"

My face burned with embarrassment. Tears were filling my eyes again. I just *hate* it when I cry in public like that.

"I . . . I can't swim."

"What?" She was looking at me as though I were nuts. "What are you talking about, Alice? I've seen you dog paddle!"

"Not in deep water."

"Water is water! If you can swim in the shallow end, you can swim in the deep end."

"Not me, Pamela. All I want to do is go home."

"Oh, just stay here. The boys will forget all about it," she said.

"No, they won't. They're looking at me like I have an eye in the middle of my forehead."

"Just laugh it off."

"Pamela, I'm still bawling!" I wailed.

Elizabeth got up and came over. Now all the boys were standing in a little group, about as far away from me as they could get.

"What's the matter?" Elizabeth whispered.

"Alice can't swim."

"What? Alice, we were in the ocean together last year!"

"Up to our waists," I said miserably. "I can't swim in deep water. I freak out."

"You want us to walk you home?" Pamela asked.

"No. I want you to go back to whatever you were doing before I made a spectacle of myself, and I'll just quietly walk off the edge of the earth. I'm embarrassed enough already."

They hung around a few more minutes to make sure that's what I wanted. Then Pamela drifted back to the diving board and Elizabeth sat down again on her towel. When I finally pulled on my shorts and left, Tom and Elizabeth were sitting side by side, and Tom was running his finger up and down her back.

I couldn't help staring. Elizabeth in her halter top bathing suit was actually sitting so close to a boy that their thighs were touching, and he was running his finger down her back. Whew! I guess she figured that having confessed to reading *Arabian Nights* was sort of like an antibiotic–the forgiveness covered all kinds of transgressions for at least ten days or so, and she was still in a period of grace.

Sometimes, when Lester has had a really bad day and

tells us about it later, he says, "I was hating life." Well, on the way home from Mark Stedmeister's, I was hating life about as much as I ever had. I didn't see how I could come back and face my friends again. Elizabeth and Pamela, yes, but not the other kids. Especially not the boys.

I had probably ruined my entire future, I decided. The story would spread all around school. I just knew that as I walked down the halls at high school, even, people would nudge each other and say, "That's the one who threw the fit at the pool." My face burned with embarrassment.

I walked up the front steps, opened the door, stepped inside, and looked at Lester who was just coming out of the kitchen with a 7–Up. Then I burst into tears. If I was going to make a fool of myself in public, I guess, I might just as well include my family.

Lester stared at me. "Was it something I said?" he joked. And when I went on sobbing, he said, "It's not the last 7–Up, Al. There's still some left."

"L-L-Lester," I sobbed, falling into his arms. "I've just ruined the r-rest of my life."

"How many people did you shoot?" he asked, patting me on the back.

I sobbed even louder. "I embarrassed myself in f-front of everyone. Everybody saw! The b-boys think I'm weird."

Lester walked me into the living room, holding me by the arms, and gently sat me down on the couch. Then, realizing that my bathing suit was soaking through my shorts, he hauled me up again and sat me down in the bean-bag chair. I sat there all scrunched up like a prune, the tears continuing to pour.

"It will be at least five minutes before the police or FBI get here, so tell me what you did," Lester insisted.

In bits and pieces, with gasps and sobs, I told him about the way the guys had grabbed me and how I'd ended up entwined in a deck chair.

I thought Lester would laugh, but he looked pretty serious.

"I had no idea you couldn't swim, Al," he said. "I just never knew that at all."

"N-n-no one d-did, not even Dad," I blurted out. "I was afraid he'd m-make me take lessons, and they just don't . . ." My voice was rising higher and higher until it sounded like a kitten's mew. ". . . don't work with me, Les. I'm hopeless."

"I don't believe that for a moment," Lester said. "Listen, Al. We'll figure something out. It doesn't have to happen again."

Of course it wouldn't happen again, I thought, because I would never go near a pool for the rest of my life. I went upstairs and sat down in my bedroom with the new furniture from Sears in it. It seemed like such a waste, the $499. What girl would ever want to come and spend a night here with a lunatic? Why spend $499 on a girl who went around collapsing in public on a folding chair, whom boys whispered about behind her back? There went my chances for the eighth-grade Semi-Formal, the Junior Snow Ball, and the

Senior Prom. For love and marriage and happiness, and maybe even a career.

When I came down for dinner that night, my first words at the table were, "I want to move."

"Oh?" said Dad, putting a big bowl of steamed shrimp on the table and a loaf of Italian bread. "Where to?"

"Where there aren't any lakes or rivers or oceans or swimming pools. Dry land as far as the eye can see," I told him.

"Nevada," said Les, peeling a shrimp. "Definitely Nevada."

I sat there glowering at my plate. "And no YWCAs, either. No health clubs."

Dad put a salad on the table, then started to cut the bread. "Well, maybe we can find you a cave somewhere."

"Yeah, Al, we'll work on it," Les told me. I was glad he didn't tell Dad what I'd told him. I picked up a piece of bread and chewed without tasting.

"In the meantime," said Dad, "Janice Sherman's going into the hospital tomorrow for a hysterectomy, Al, and I wondered if you'd be willing to go with me to see her in a few days."

I knew that an "ectomy" means something's taken out, like an appendix, but a hysterectomy?

"What's missing?" I asked.

"Her uterus, Al. It's a common operation, but Janice is a little young for it, I guess, and she's feeling kind of down."

"What am *I* suppose to do? Give her mine?" I quipped. I wasn't feeling sorry for anybody but myself.

"Oh, you might just stop by her room with me. We'll pick up some flowers. The truth is, I'd feel a little more comfortable having a female along. It might be embarrassing talking to her about it by myself."

It's amazing what a change it makes in the way you feel just knowing somebody needs you.

A few days later we went to see Janice. I didn't like Holy Cross Hospital any better than I had when I went to see my sixth-grade teacher, Mrs. Plotkin, after her heart attack; but it wasn't so bad with Dad along.

We found her room, Dad gave a little knock on the door, and we went in—me with a box of chocolates and Dad with the flowers. I don't think I'd ever seen Janice without her makeup, and she looked thinner and paler than she had before, but otherwise okay.

"How's my favorite assistant manager?" Dad asked, which doesn't mean a whole lot because she's his *only* assistant manager.

Janice forced a smile. "As well as can be expected, I guess," she said.

"We brought you some chocolate turtles," I told her. "Your favorite."

"Thanks, Alice. Just put them there on the night table, will you? And the flowers are lovely."

There was already another box of turtles and at least

three other bouquets, but I figured the more the better to make up for a missing uterus.

"I called the hospital this morning to see how you were doing, and the nurse said you were coming along fine," Dad said, sitting down in the one chair. I leaned against the window sill.

"Well, it's not the nurse who's here in bed, it's me," said Janice. "It's the thought of it that's hard to get used to, I guess. This is something I never expected at all. Like an . . . amputation."

"I can understand that," I said. "Pamela got gum in her hair last spring and had to have her hair cut off. It used to be so long she could sit on it. Now it's a short feather cut, and she feels naked."

There was silence in the room, and then Dad quickly started a story about something that happened at work. I didn't know what I'd said that was wrong, but I knew enough not to open my mouth again until we said good-bye.

"Al," Dad told me on the way back out to the car. "Couldn't you have thought of something a little more sympathetic to say to Janice? I know you meant well, but . . ."

I was puzzled. "What was wrong with it? I really want to know."

"You made it sound as though her operation wasn't too much different from a haircut. Janice can't ever bear children now, you know."

"But she's not married anyway!"

"And this just emphasizes the fact," he said.

I thought about that all the way home. I wondered if anyone had made thoughtless remarks to my mother when she was in the hospital. I hoped not. Dad says that unless you've lost your uterus, you probably can't even imagine what it's like. I say that unless you've lost three feet of blond hair, or have a fear of deep water, you can't imagine that, either.

The fact is, I guess, *no*body knows what it's like to be in a certain situation except the one who's in it. But just as there was a big difference between what happened to Janice and what happened to Pamela, there was a big difference between what had happened to them and what was happening to me. There wasn't a thing they could do about their situations; they had to deal with them after they happened. There was plenty I could do about mine, but I was too afraid to try, and that got me thinking.

Nobody was asking me to bungee jump, after all. Nobody was asking me to lie down in the middle of a highway or race a train to a crossing. All I was expected to do was what millions of other people do on a hot summer day, yet I just couldn't seem to get up my nerve. That's why *no* one could convince me to go back to Mark's the next day or the next or the next, and I was sure I would go the rest of my life without putting on a bathing suit again.

$\mathcal{A}$ MATTER OF TRUST

$\mathcal{P}$atrick came back from Banff and brought me a pair of earrings with tiny jade stones in them.

"To match your eyes," he said, and kissed me. I guess we were really a couple again. You could say we were "going together." For the next two minutes, anyway, until I told him about my deep-water fear.

"How was Canada?" I asked.

"Big," he said.

I wanted to throw my arms around his neck and say, *Promise you'll still like me after you find out what happened at Mark's pool!*

What I said was, "I made a jerk of myself at Mark's the other day."

He put one arm around my shoulder as we walked to High's for a cone. "What'd you do? Fall off the diving board or something?"

"Patrick, I can't even *get* on the diving board." I took a deep breath. "I'm afraid of deep water. I never told any of the other kids before. The guys tried to throw me in, and I freaked out."

"What'd you do? Slug 'em?"

"I started crying and held onto a collapsible chair."

I could tell by the way his eyebrows moved that he was trying to imagine it.

"I feel so dumb," I told him.

"You need swimming lessons."

"In your dreams."

"Join a health club."

"That's even worse."

"You going to spend the rest of your life on land?" he asked.

"If God wanted me to swim, he would have given me gills," I answered. I knew I sounded too cool. Too controlled. Only Lester had seen how upset I really was. I wasn't about to cry in front of Patrick. "I . . . I know how you had plans for us to try out for the swim team together," I added.

Patrick shrugged. "Well, there'll be other things we can do," he told me, but I could tell he was disappointed.

For the rest of the week, the weather was unusually muggy for the end of August. Just moving across the room could make you hot, and even the leaves on the trees seemed to hang limp and thirsty. Patrick and all the other kids in our crowd practically lived at Mark Stedmeister's. They went every afternoon and sometimes evenings as well.

Elizabeth was wearing Tom Perona's ID bracelet again, the one he'd asked to have back the summer after sixth grade, when he broke up with Elizabeth for a girl who would kiss. He must have decided that Elizabeth kissed just fine.

She wouldn't stop talking about it, either. Elizabeth, the girl who wouldn't discuss bodies, now wouldn't shut up when it came to kisses. She described each kiss as though it were a pineapple upside-down cake–every delicious crumb, right up to the cherries on top.

I hung around with Elizabeth and Pamela in the mornings, but in the afternoons when they went to the pool, I stayed home and made excuses: it was my period; I was getting a cold; my suit didn't fit. What hurt was that they just went without me. I was as miserable as I could ever remember.

Whenever Patrick came over and we sat out on the swing together, we seemed to talk about other things just so long, and then it always got back to swimming.

"Why *don't* you take lessons, Alice?" he'd end up saying. "You'll never get over your fear unless you do."

"It's the fear that's keeping me from swimming lessons, don't you understand?" I'd tell him. "If I was brave enough to take swimming lessons in the first place, I'd be brave enough to go in the deep end."

"So you're never going swimming for the rest of your life?" he asked finally.

"That's the plan," I said, and when my voice trembled, he reached over and held my hand. That should have helped, but it didn't.

"Hey, Al," Lester said that evening, when I was sitting on the front steps alone. "It's the last week of vacation. Live it up."

"I am," I said frowning, and took another angry bite of peach.

"Where are all your friends?"

"Where do you think?" I muttered, and threw the peach pit about as hard as I could into the bushes.

As I lay in bed that night staring up at the ceiling, a thought that had been chewing on me suddenly nipped hard enough to be recognized: if I didn't overcome this fear now, it would be the first of many. I would have given in, so it would be easier to give in the next time I was afraid of something. Then the next.

What if I decided I was too afraid to learn to drive? The beltway scares the daylights out of me. Maybe I should give up that idea.

What if I decided I was too afraid to go to the dentist? To take chemistry in high school? Maybe I'd decide I was too scared to have babies and keep putting it off until I was too old, or had to have a hysterectomy like Janice Sherman. Maybe I'd decide I was afraid to fly. To ski. To take a lot of chances that made the difference between being alive and being dead.

I could feel my sweat on the sheet beneath me—the cold hard sweat that comes from fear—but I knew I was going to do something about it. I didn't know what, but I'd made up my mind that it would be *something.* And in that very moment of deciding, along with the cold sweat and the terror, there was a strange sort of calm. For the first time I realized it was not only the deep water I feared; it was making the decision. Once I'd done that, the hardest part was over.

Until the next morning, that is. I was awakened out of a deep sleep by somebody moving my foot. It was Lester.

"Hey, Al. Rise and shine. No work today. Big date," he said.

"What?"

"Come on. My treat."

"What are you talking about?"

"Surprise. Can't tell."

I got up and washed my face.

"Eat something," Lester said.

It was nine-thirty, and Dad had long since left. I couldn't decide between breakfast or lunch, so I ate a bowl of Rice Chex while I heated a slice of pizza. By the time I'd finished breakfast, I was a little bit excited about what Lester had planned. I knew he was just trying to be kind because I was feeling so left out of things, but I decided to take whatever little bit of kindness I could get.

"Okay, go put on your swimsuit," Lester said.

"Oh, no!" The excitement disappeared like snow on a summer day.

"Just you and me. Not another soul around."

"Where?"

"The Harkinses' backyard. they have a pool, and they're out of town for the week. Crystal wouldn't mind if we used it."

"Les, I . . . I *want* to, but I can't!"

"Why, Al?"

"I'm just scared. I'm terrified, in fact! You'll say you're going to hold me up but you won't. I know you."

Lester didn't laugh. He really seemed to be studying me for a long time. Then he said, "Come on out in back."

We went out the back door and Lester told me to stand on the top step. He went down to the bottom.

"Turn around and face the house," he said.

I turned around, my back to him.

"Now fall backward," Lester told me.

"Are you nuts?" I looked at him over my shoulder. "I'll break my neck!"

"You would if I didn't catch you, but I will. You *know* I will. Just put your arms down at your sides, relax, and fall straight backward."

"Les, if you let me fall . . .!"

"*Trust* me, Al. For once, just trust me."

I faced the door again. "Are you ready? Are your arms out?" I called.

"I'm ready, Al."

I closed my eyes. "I'm coming, Lester," I said, but I didn't move. "I can't," I wailed.

"Listen. Have I ever let you down big? Even one time?"

I could think of a lot of little times but nothing life threatening. "No," I confessed.

"Try it, Al. Just let yourself go. I'm right here."

I sighed. "Okay, Lester. Ready? Here I come."

I closed my eyes and fell straight back, and Lester caught me and stood me back up.

"Do it again," he said.

I fell again.

"Again."

When I'd done it about ten times, Lester said, "I will no more let go of you in the water than I would let you fall on your back."

I sucked in my breath. "Promise?"

"Absolutely."

I had to admit I was feeling a little bit excited along with the terror. I put on my suit, and we drove to the Harkinses' home. I hadn't seen much of Crystal since June, but I guessed she and Les must still talk on the phone. There was a high fence around the backyard, but Lester knew how to get in, and closed the gate after us. It was like a private club—a large patio with a pool beside it and a yard beyond.

I had no trouble getting into the shallow end, of course, and even proving to myself and Lester that I could stay up by dog-paddling. I could even get myself from one side of the pool to the other without putting my foot down once, because I knew that at any minute I could if I wanted.

"Now let me show you how easy it is in the deep end," said Lester.

My fear rose again. "I can't!"

"I didn't say a word about you," he said. "Just watch."

I walked to the deep end with him. "I'm going to jump in, and without even trying, without moving my arms one inch, I will pop right back up again," he said. "All I have to do is take a big gulp of air, and my lungs become a floatation device."

Lester went to the side of the pool, jumped in with his legs together and his arms straight down at his sides. Just as he said, he sank right to the bottom and popped back up to the surface again.

He shook the water from his head and swam over to the side. "See, Al? See how quickly I came back up without even trying?"

"That's *you*, Lester, it's not me. If it's all that easy, how come people drown? How come people fall in, never to be seen again?"

"Because they panic, or there's a strong current that pulls them under, or because they hit their head on something–all kinds of reasons, but none that have anything to do with you. Just take a big breath before you jump."

"Panic has everything to do with me," I said. "My middle name is panic. Lester, I don't care how easily you pop to the surface; I'll panic and drown."

"Al, watch." Lester was being more patient than I had ever seen him before. He crawled out, went over to the side of the pool, and came back with a vacuum pole.

"I'm going to take a big breath and jump in the deep end. No matter how hard I try to stay down there, you'll have to hold me down. Now watch."

He jumped in again, and this time when he got to the bottom, he used his hands and kept aiming at the floor of the swimming pool, tilting his body down, kicking his feet to stay there. But just as he said, he kept rising to the surface.

He popped up and took a breath. "Once I get down there, hold me down with the pole for a few seconds," he said, treading water.

Timidly, I watched until he was at the bottom, then I put the pole in the water and pressed down on his shoulder. Even then, his body kept popping out around it, starting to rise, and I had to push him some more. I kept him down for five seconds, then let him up.

"I'm still scared, Lester," I said. "You might as well give up on me."

"Okay. Plan B," said Lester. "Let's go back to the shallow end."

We walked back to the three-foot water and stood on the edge.

"Hold your nose with one hand and hold onto me with the other, and we'll jump together," Lester said.

That was easy. We jumped in, holding hands, and didn't even go under. Lester didn't let go of my hand for a second.

"Okay, four feet," Lester said when we climbed out again.

That was a little more scary, but he let me stand on the shallow side, so that in a pinch I could balance on my toes. We jumped, and again Lester never let go of my hand.

"Good!" said Lester. "Al, you're doing great. Now five feet."

I actually wasn't as scared of five feet as four feet, because I realized how close we were to the edge of the pool. Again we jumped, and it took longer for my feet to touch the bottom. The water thrubbed in my ears, and for a moment I felt panicky, but Lester had a strong hold on my hand, and a moment later we both popped to the surface. He held me up with one arm.

We did six feet, then seven, and each time Lester was there for me—right there holding me up.

"Break time!" Lester said, so we just sat on the edge by the deep end and dangled our feet in the water. I was feeling so proud of myself I was ready to burst. Once Lester even slipped down into the water and horsed around, right under my feet, so that I could touch the top of his head. The water didn't seem so deep, somehow, when it was only a foot or so over the top of Lester's head.

"Next step," Lester said finally, and swam over to the corner where I was sitting. "Turn around, Al, and lower yourself into the pool, but keep holding onto the edge."

"L-Lester," I said shakily.

"Trust me?"

I swallowed. "Okay."

I turned around and crawled in, clinging to the rim like a shipwrecked passenger.

"Now here's what we do," Lester said, moving me along the edge of the pool until I was about two feet away from the corner, but still holding on. He put out his long arms and legs, making a triangular pen in that corner of the pool and began treading water. "I want you to dog-paddle from where you are right now, Al, to my left hand over here. It'll be about two strokes. At any time, you can reach out and grab the side of the pool if you want to. It's right there. And you can't come out any farther than I am."

It was part scary and part silly. It was like being in a playpen, actually, with hardly enough room to move. I waited until I got up my nerve, then leaned forward in the water and dog-paddled, lunging out ahead of me and grabbing the edge of the pool.

"Bravo!" said Lester, even though I had only been detached for about a second. "You did it, Al! Do it again."

I smiled triumphantly, and this time did about three seconds worth of dog-paddling."

"Okay, back up a little this time, and swim the corner again."

Backing up made the distance about twice as long, but with Lester out there as a fence, keeping me in the corner, I felt safe, and I did it.

I shrieked with happiness. The whole pool seemed different somehow as I got to know this one little corner, this one small space with Lester there to keep me from sinking.

From then on, it was easy. I finally succeeded in swimming across the entire width of the deep end, Lester beside me all the way, and had just started to go back again when the gate opened, and two policemen entered the yard.

I was so startled I turned completely around and went back. I didn't even know I could do that.

"Good morning," one of the policemen said, from the patio.

"Good morning," said Lester.

I climbed out and reached for my towel.

"You the people who live here?" asked the second officer.

"No. The pool belongs to a friend of mine, and she doesn't care if we use it," Lester said.

"Well, we received a call from a neighbor about someone entering the premises, and I guess I'll need proof that you know the owner," the policeman said.

Lester swam over to the shallow end. "You mean I have to have a note or something? The Harkinses are in Maine! Crystal always told me that I was welcome to use her pool. I'm teaching my sister to swim."

The officers looked doubtful.

Just then a woman appeared at the gate.

"Are you the neighbor who made the call, ma'am?" the first officer asked.

"Yes, I did. I saw this man taking this young girl in here and closing the gate, and I knew the Harkinses were gone, and . . ."

"He's my brother," I said quickly.

"Your name?" asked one of the policemen.

"Alice McKinley. This is Lester."

"Well, we'll just see about this," said the neighbor. "I'll call the Harkinses myself." And she headed back toward her own house.

The officers came on in and sat down on the deck chairs.

"Nice pool," said one.

"Good place to be on a day like this," said the other.

I sat down on the other side of the pool across from the policemen and wondered if they'd shoot me if I tried to run. They asked where I went to school and where Lester went to college and how long we'd lived in Silver Spring. Then the neighbor came back.

"I talked to Crystal," she told us, "and she said she never heard of a Lester McKinley before in her life."

"What . . .?" Lester stared, almost speechless. "I've been *dating* the girl!"

"Not for the past two months you haven't," the neighbor declared. "Actually, Crystal said you haven't even written or called since she went to Maine, and she wouldn't mind seeing you hauled off to jail for a couple of hours. She wouldn't want anything to happen to Alice, though, so she said you can stay as long as Alice is with you."

"She knows him," one officer said to the other.

"And if I see you here with any other girl, I'm supposed to call the police immediately," the neighbor went on.

"I'd say she knows him pretty well," the other officer said. He smiled down at me. "How's the lesson coming?"

I can't think what got into me. Knowing that there were two policemen there to rescue me, plus Lester, I guess, I walked over to the side of the pool.

"Watch!" I told them.

And then, my heart thumping hard, I held my nose and jumped back into the deep end.

Thrub, thrub, thrub, went the water in my ears. I knew it would be only a second or two before my feet touched bottom, and after that I would pop to the surface like a cork.

I popped and immediately began dog-paddling, hardly able to see through the wet hair over my face, gasping and panting, but I could hear the officers cheering me on.

After we had the pool to ourselves again, there was no holding me back. I dog-paddled the width of the pool again, then the length, then tried the swimming stroke Lester taught me, but I kept my head above water. It worked.

"Lester," I said, "before we go home, I want to jump off the diving board."

"What?" Even Lester was surprised.

"I don't want to learn to dive right now. I don't even care if I don't know any fancy strokes. I just want to be able to jump off the diving board and prove that I'll come right up again."

So Lester stayed down in the deep end near the place I would land, and I climbed the ladder. This was *really* scary. I didn't realize just how nervous I would be. Slowly I walked out to the end of the bouncy board. I held my nose, took a deep breath, and jumped.

It was the longest moment of my life—probably only two seconds, but it felt like thirty. I could hear the gluggle of water in my ears as I went down, down, down, and then . . . *whoosh*! I felt myself begin to rise, and I was home free.

After that Lester taught me how to rise faster from the

bottom by putting my hands straight up over my head, then bringing them down to my sides. I could actually control myself under water. If I pushed down on it, I popped to the surface. If I pushed up against it, I stayed under longer. It was up to me. I was the boss.

There was one more thing to do before we called it a day. I wanted Lester to pick me up and throw me in the deep end like the boys might do to me if I ever went back to Mark's pool. I wanted to know what it felt like. I wanted to know if I could handle it.

"You sure of this, Al?" he said. "You might land upside down. You might have to turn yourself around in the water."

"I can do that," I said.

Lester picked me up and walked over to the side, then threw me in the seven-foot water. I went in upside down, but when I reached the bottom, I put my hands together like he had shown me, cutting the water like a knife, bringing them down to my sides again, and shot right up to the surface. I had already learned to trust Lester, and now I was learning to trust myself! Again he tossed me in, sideways, backward, and I didn't drown once.

"Lester," I said, as we headed home at last. "This was about the best day of my life. I was so afraid before, and suddenly I can wake up in the mornings and not have to worry anymore." I reached over and grabbed his arm. "You're really, really great!"

"I only did it so if you ever fall in a river, I won't have to ruin my clothes getting you out," he said.

$\mathcal{L}$UCK

$\mathcal{I}$ had to call Aunt Sally, of course, and tell her.

"Why, Alice, that's wonderful," she said. "Marie would be so proud of you. She was an excellent swimmer, you know."

"So I've heard."

According to a note on the table, Dad picked up Miss Summers after he'd finished at the Melody Inn and gone to a concert at Wolf Trap. When he got back that night, I told him what a terrific day this had been for me.

I could tell that Dad was really shocked.

"Al, I had no idea! Are you *sure* you couldn't swim in deep water?" he kept asking.

"Trust me," I said, sounding like Lester.

"If Marie knew I let you get to thirteen, hanging around pools and not even knowing how to swim. . . ."

"You've had a lot on your mind, Dad, these past thirteen years. You're doing okay," I told him.

"What bothers me is what else I might have overlooked. What else do you need to learn to do?" he went on.

"How long a list do you want?" I replied. "I need to learn to kiss with my lips just touching, for starters."

"Oh, for Pete's sake, Al. . . ."

"Lester," I said, turning around, "let me practice on you."

"Bug off. Enough is enough."

"Just once! I just want to learn how to touch and back off and touch and back off. . . ."

"Practice on your hand! Practice on a book! Kiss the door of the refrigerator! When the time comes, you'll do just fine."

The gang was getting together at Mark Stedmeister's on Labor Day weekend for one last fling.

When I showed up at Mark's that Saturday afternoon, I could tell the kids were surprised to see me. The boys all said a polite "Hi," keeping their distance, but Patrick whooped and waved to me from the water.

I waved back, and slipped off my shorts, just like nothing had ever happened. I ate a couple potato chips and talked with Jill and Karen. I spread my towel out on the cement between Elizabeth and Pamela, and then, just as though I did it every day, I walked down to the deep end, over to the diving board.

For a moment no one seemed to notice. Then I heard Elizabeth say, "My gosh! Alice is on the diving board!" And everyone turned.

I had hoped to jump and be in the water before anyone noticed, because I wanted a practice jump first, but now everyone had stopped talking and was looking in my direction. Patrick, paddling around below, moved out of the way.

I walked right to the end of the board, my heart pounding like crazy. Everyone looked different up here–a lot farther down in the water. The diving board seemed higher than the one at the Harkinses, too. But I remembered that water is water is water, whether it's four-feet deep or fifty, and that I could trust my body to do its thing.

You swim like a fish, I told myself. And then, *You swim just like Mom.*

Walking to the end of the board, I held my nose, then jumped feet first, keeping my legs together the way Lester taught me so I'd slice the water cleanly, my other arm up over my head.

Whum! Water drubbed in my ears as I went down, down, down. I put my other hand up over my head, too, then brought my arms swiftly down to my sides.

Whop! I shot up to the surface and emerged to the sound of clapping and cheering.

"Way to go, Alice!" yelled Brian.

"She did it!" came Pamela's astonished cry.

"I thought you couldn't swim," said Mark Stedmeister, as I dog-paddled over to Patrick along the side.

"I learned," I told him.

"What happened?" asked Patrick. "How did you do it?"

"Lester taught me," I said. "That's what brothers are for."

"Well, you looked really nice up there," Patrick said, and leaned over and kissed me, our faces wet and hair hanging down over our eyes. It wasn't the way I'd fantasized, but a kiss is a kiss is a kiss, I told myself.

I guess, seeing how quickly I went from a non-swimmer to jumping off the diving board, I shouldn't have been surprised that Elizabeth was changing, too; but since she had gone to confession she had changed right before my eyes. All the priest told her, I understood, was that it was okay to be curious, and boy was she curious. About kissing. About flirting. She was curious about lying side by side on a towel with Tom Perona, Tom's arm over her back.

"It didn't take *her* long to get the hang of eighth grade, and school hasn't even started yet!" Pamela observed.

"It's amazing, isn't it? All three of us are back to dating the same boys we were seeing in sixth grade," I said, as Pamela and I went into Mark's house to use the bathroom.

"Well, not quite," Pamela said, going into the bathroom first and shutting the door.

"What do you mean?" I called.

She didn't answer at first, but when the toilet flushed and she opened the door, she said, "I think I'm going to break up with Mark."

I stared. "What? You've been going with Mark ever since I can remember! You've been coming to his house to swim all summer."

"I know, but I'd sort of like to play the field."

"Who else is there?"

"Well, there's Brian, for one."

I grabbed her by the shoulders. "Pamela, he's the one who put gum in your hair!"

She grinned sheepishly. "Crazy, isn't it?"

I leaned weakly against the door frame. "When are you going to tell Mark?"

"Tonight."

"Oh, lordy," I said. I sounded like Aunt Sally.

I went into the bathroom, forgot why I was there, and walked right out again. Here we were at the Stedmeisters'. Mark's mom had fixed hot dogs and potato salad, and somebody had brought a German chocolate cake. We were all celebrating a glorious summer and the start of eighth grade, and after everyone left, Mark was going to get it right between the eyes.

"Can't you at least wait until school starts?" I suggested.

"Alice, it's important to start eighth grade as someone's girlfriend. I mean, I don't want to be going with Mark one day and Brian the next. I want people to see us as a couple right from the start."

"You mean you want the other girls to know that Brian belongs to you."

"Something like that," Pamela told me.

"What are you going to tell Mark? What reason can you give?"

"That it's time to go out with other people, but I still want us to be friends."

Fat chance, I thought.

Life is weird. All summer—all my life, practically—I've

been worrying about my secret fear of deep water; it was always a lump in the back of my throat. And suddenly it's the last thing on my mind, and all I can think about on Labor Day weekend is that Mark is having the time of his life, and a couple hours from now he'll be devastated.

I tried not to look at him, but my eyes kept drifting over there anyway. Now that I was paying attention, though, I noticed how Pamela was hanging around Brian, laughing when he teased her, egging him on. It was so obvious she was making a play for him that I wondered why I hadn't noticed before.

And then Mark did the most incredibly stupid thing I have ever seen in my life. Every so often, boys just go berserk momentarily. Some hormone gets out of whack, and they are temporarily deranged. Because we were all standing around the picnic table in one corner of the Stedmeisters' deck, eating off paper plates, and suddenly Mark took his plate over to where Pamela was talking with Brian, pulled open the back of her elastic bikini bottom, and dumped his potato salad in her pants.

Everyone gasped.

Pamela didn't even scream. She just turned around with this incredulous look, and threw her cup of Pepsi in Mark's face. Then she walked, as gracefully as she could under the circumstances, toward the house.

Mark spluttered and tried to laugh it off. Everyone was standing around in embarrassed silence. I was in awe. All my life I've been convinced I've done some of the stu-

pidest things known to mankind, but I had just wit-
nessed something worse.

"Hey, Mark, that was really dumb," Patrick said finally.
"She's really ticked."

"Oh, heck, it was all a joke," Mark said. Then he yelled,
"Hey Pamela, I'm sorry. Come back."

And when there was no answer, he laughed and yelled,
"Hey, c'mon, and I'll help get the potato salad out."

A door slammed somewhere inside, rattling the whole
house, and Mrs. Stedmeister glanced out the window, her
face puzzled, then disappeared again.

Elizabeth and I went inside to help Pamela. She was in
the bathroom, taking clumps of potato salad out of her
bathing suit and dropping them down the toilet. I knew
why she was taking it so calmly. Fate had just handed her a
reason for breaking up with Mark–handed it to her on a
paper platter.

We followed her out to the pool then, where she picked
up her towel.

"Walk me home, Brian?" she said.

Mark stared speechless. Brian looked confused.

"Uh . . . sure," he said. "So long, everybody. Nice party,
Mark. See you in school." And he walked off into the sun-
set with Mark's girl. *Ex*-girl.

The party broke up shortly after that. Elizabeth and Jill
and Karen and I helped pick up all the dirty plates and cups
and throw them in the trash, but Mark stood there dazed,
looking out after Pamela.

Tom walked Elizabeth home, and Patrick came home with me. As soon as we were out of Mark's yard, I said, "Pamela's broken up with Mark."

"She has? Why?" asked Patrick.

I stopped and faced him. There are times I think boys take Stupid Pills every morning to make them say the things they do.

"Patrick, didn't you see what Mark *did* to her?"

"Yeah, but I think she must have been thinking about breaking up with him even before," Patrick said. "I think that's the reason Mark dropped the salad in her suit in the first place."

Patrick was smarter than I'd thought.

Later that evening I got a wild thought. I called Pamela.

"Just out of curiosity, Pamela, did you get a letter a week or so ago about St. Jude?"

"Yes," said Pamela. "How did you know?"

"Because Elizabeth and I each got one. I think Donald Sheavers sent them. What did you do with yours?"

"I don't know. I suppose it's around here someplace. Why?"

"Just curious," I told her.

We had each gotten a letter. I was so afraid to take chances, I'd sent mine on, as it said, and I learned to jump in deep water.

Pamela had misplaced hers and found a good reason to break up with Mark Stedmeister.

Elizabeth's mother had thrown hers in the trash, and

Elizabeth learned to kiss. All three of us had done something different with our letters, yet good luck had come to all.

There was a phone call for me that evening. Lester yelled to me from downstairs, and I took it up in the hall. It was Miss Summers.

"I just wanted to say hi, Alice, and to thank you for the letter about St. Jude."

I swallowed.

"I'm not sure how I feel about luck coming from a letter, so I didn't send it on, but I wanted to thank you for thinking of me."

"Oh, it's okay," I said. "I just didn't know what else to do with it, but I think Dad was sort of angry that I sent it to you."

"He was? Why?"

"I . . . well . . . uh . . . I guess he doesn't believe much in luck. He thinks we make our own luck."

"I'm sure he's right. Anyway, I'm going to miss having you in my seventh-grade class this year. But I'm sure we'll be seeing each other from time to time."

"I hope so," I told her.

After I hung up, I went to Lester.

"Does 'from time to time' mean a lot or a little?" I asked.

"What the heck are you talking about, Al?"

I told him what Miss Summers had said.

"I think it's a cagey response from an unattached woman who doesn't want to presume either too much or too little," Lester told me.

Which didn't tell me a whole lot, one way or another.

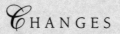CHANGES

$\mathcal{M}$ost of the stores were having big sales on Labor Day, so Dad kept the Melody Inn open, and I put in another three hours to help out.

September had come to Maryland with all sorts of changes. I was swimming, Elizabeth was kissing, Pamela was going with Brian, Janice Sherman would be coming back to work in a few weeks without her uterus, and Lester would soon be celebrating his twenty-first birthday.

"I remember too well when *I* was twenty-one. I wouldn't be twenty-one again for anything," said Dad.

"You're joking," said Lester. "I thought everyone wanted to stay twenty-one forever."

"Nope. Twenty-eight, maybe, or thirty-five. Forty, even. But not those early twenties. Too much energy going to waste."

The other thing that happened was that Loretta Jenkins, who runs the Gift Shoppe at the Melody Inn, came to work engaged to be married within a few days. It was only a couple months ago she'd been chasing Lester.

"Congratulations," I said. "Who's the guy?"

"A bartender I met at a club," she told me. "He's really cute."

The big news, though, was that she was pregnant. I couldn't believe it. Neither could Lester. We were both probably thinking of the times she had asked him out, but he always made excuses. When Dad told him the news, Lester folded his hands, lifted his eyes to the heavens, and said, "Thank you, thank you, thank you that I did not go camping with Loretta Jenkins."

"What is it with young people today?" Dad fumed. "Everyone's in such a blamed hurry. Do this! Try that! Experience everything as though there's no tomorrow. Nobody savors anything anymore."

Dad was stressed out, and I knew it. With Janice home recuperating and Loretta throwing up in the john, he was carrying a triple load. I was glad I could help him out that Monday, and Lester even came by after he finished at Maytag to give Dad a hand. We weren't surprised, though, when Dad told us to go home after the store closed, and he'd do the receipts.

"Tell you what," Les said to me. "If we go out to eat, neither of us has to cook, so what about some Thai food? I know a little place in Kensington, and we'll order extra so Dad can have something to heat up when he gets home."

We drove to Kensington, and the waiter must have thought we were dating, because he led us to an adjoining room half filled with plants where, if we *had* been a dating couple, we could have practiced kissing like Elizabeth and Tom Perona had been doing.

"Guess what, Lester, the waiter thinks we're in love," I told him.

Lester rolled his eyes and opened the menu.

"Too bad I'm not Marilyn or Crystal," I said. "If you had to choose one or the other right this very minute, who would you pick?"

He shrugged. "They both have different qualities."

"You haven't seen much of Crystal lately," I told him.

"So I'm in my Marilyn mood," Lester answered. "Open the menu, Al, and pick something."

The waiter had placed me against the wall where I could see through the plants into the main room of the restaurant, but Lester was facing me and the wall.

"Too bad you don't have anything better to look at," I quipped. "Want me to try to be Crystal Harkins for the evening and talk Bach?"

"I want you to figure out what you're having to eat and quit yapping," he told me.

I looked at the menu, but there wasn't anything I recognized. Half the food was served with lemon grass, whatever that was. I imagined having to get down on my hands and knees to eat it.

"Order for me, huh?" I said. "I can't even pronounce this stuff."

So Lester ordered strips of beef on lemon grass, shrimp on skewers, and spring rolls. We ate crab soup and garlic chicken, and the kind of rice that sticks together when you eat it with chopsticks.

I had just asked Lester what he remembered of eighth grade—whether it was better or worse than seventh—when I saw a couple come in the front door of the restaurant and wait to be seated, and my heart almost jumped through my chest. It was Miss Summers and a man, and it wasn't Dad.

For a moment I didn't think I could breathe.

"What's the matter, Al? Something stuck in your throat?" Lester asked, ready to spring to his feet and try the Heimlich maneuver.

"Les," I said weakly, "it's Miss Summers with another man."

Lester stopped chewing. "You sure?"

"Turn around and look."

"Don't be dumb. And quit staring."

I could no more quit staring than I could swallow. What would I do if the waiter seated them in here? What would I say?

The head water motioned them to a table in the other room, however, behind the row of plants that separated us from them. I could just see them from time to time if they leaned forward or something. They were too far away for me to hear anything.

My eyes filled with tears.

"Al, for Pete's sake . . .!"

"She's dating someone *else,* Lester!"

"Well, that's her business. She's not engaged to Dad, you know."

I swallowed. Then swallowed again. "But I wanted them to marry. . . ."

"Well, then, quit jumping to conclusions. She's here with another man, and you've got her breaking up with Dad already. Maybe it's her uncle. Her brother . . ."

"Not the way he was guiding her to a table with one hand on her waist, Lester," I told him.

"Even brothers do that now and then," said Lester, and went on eating.

"Les, please turn around and tell me what you think."

"No! Do I have to beat you over the head, Al? Don't embarrass me."

"What will we tell Dad?"

This time Lester put down his fork and looked me straight in the eye. "Al, listen to me. You've got to do something that could be even harder for you than jumping in that pool. You've got to promise not to say one word about this to Dad. Understood? I mean *nothing*! Not even a hint."

I blew my nose.

"This guy could be an old friend, a relative, could be almost anyone at all. If you start suspicions in Dad's head, you could get them quarreling and breaking up. If she's dating someone else, Dad will find out eventually. You can't go around bursting people's bubbles, especially when it could all turn out to be a mistake."

Lester went on talking about the food, but I hardly heard. There was something going on between the man and Miss Summers, all right, because they looked very serious. Hardly smiled at all except at the waiter. When Miss Summers tended to look my way, I moved so that she couldn't see me behind the plants, and because she was sitting sideways to me, she didn't look over often.

But she was leaning forward talking to the man. He was a younger man than Dad—by a few years, anyway. Taller, better built. Not especially good looking, but I suppose some women would think he was handsome. Sort of heavy eyelids, thick brows. Craggy-looking.

He seemed to be listening intently to her, and Miss Summers looked very earnest. Then she would listen and the man would talk and look earnest.

"Let's go," I heard Lester saying at last. "You're not eating a thing, and you're not listening to me, either. I'll ask the waiter to wrap it up."

"I'm sorry."

The waiter brought the check, and put all the stuff we didn't eat into little boxes. All the way home in the car, tears rolled down my cheeks for Dad. Lester didn't say very much, and I knew he was thinking about Dad, too.

We parked in the driveway. Dad was already home. I started to get out, but Lester put his arm across my chest to stop me. "Remember," he said. "Not one word to Dad. I mean it, Al! No matter how much you're tempted or how right it seems, it's not."

We went inside.

"Supper, Dad!" Lester sang out. "How about some Thai food?"

Dad was lying down on the couch, his feet hanging off the side so he wouldn't get the cushions dirty.

"I'm beat," he said. "You couldn't have picked a better night. Heat it in the microwave for me, would you, and I'll eat it here in the living room."

He sat up slowly. "If I don't get some extra help at the store, I'm going to need a stay in the hospital."

I gave him a hug. "I love you, Dad," I said. "No matter what happens."

Dad squeezed my arm. "I love you, too, Al, but what's that supposed to mean?"

I caught Lester frowning at me from the hallway. "Just that I know how hard you're working, and I'm afraid you might get sick or something."

"Janice will be back half-time one of these days. I'll survive," he said.

I cried my eyes out in bed that night—for Dad, for me, for everything I had hoped would happen in the future but probably wouldn't now. I was glad I wasn't going to have Miss Summers for English, because I didn't know what I would say to her if I did. *I just want you to know you have really loused up our lives, and it would have been better if Dad had never met you.* That's what I wanted to say.

Except that I was the one responsible. I was the one who

had invited her to the *Messiah* sing-along last December. Lester was right. I should stay out of Dad's love life and let him marry who he wants. Even Janice Sherman without her uterus, if he wants, except he never even wanted to marry Janice *with* her uterus.

It was the first time in my life I realized that it's harder to see someone close to you go through pain than it is to feel it yourself. Lester was right about something else: it was going to take a lot more courage to stand on the sidelines and let things take their course between Dad and Miss Summers than it was to climb that ladder at the swimming pool and jump off the diving board.

If Mom were here, she'd know how to handle it, I thought. Then I realized that if Mom were here, Dad wouldn't be interested in Miss Summers. Or would he? My head was almost too confused to sleep.

School began the next day. Lester left for an early class at the university, so I had Dad all to myself. He made what he calls a "power breakfast" for us—a stack of thin buckwheat pancakes alternating with ricotta cheese and orange marmalade.

"Question," I said as I dug in. "I know that married people fall out of love sometimes and get divorced, but does it ever happen that someone who's happily married is still attracted to somebody else?"

"Of course," said Dad, pouring himself a cup of coffee. "Happens all the time."

I stared. "Even . . . with you . . . when Mom was alive?"

"Sure."

"Dad . . .!" I was growing up too fast and learning things I didn't want to know.

"Well, you asked."

"You mean you were going out with other women?"

"Of course not."

"But . . . you might have been happier with someone else?"

"Sure!"

The warm little bubble I'd carried around with me ever since I can remember seemed to have been popped by a cold wind.

But Dad was giving me a quizzical smile. "Listen, sweetheart, I dated six women before I met your mother, and there were probably two billion women in the world at that particular time. Just looking at it mathematically, there were probably a million I might have been happier with or who suited me better than Marie."

That didn't help a bit. "Then why . . .?"

"Why did I marry her? Because I knew that she was a woman I could love—that I *did* love. And since I couldn't possibly date all the other women I'd be meeting in my life-time, why not settle on her? I was committed to the marriage, Al. That's what makes the difference."

And suddenly my warm fuzzy feeling was back again, my armor for the first day of eighth grade, and all the other firsts I'd have in my life. But it wasn't just what Dad had said. It was the feeling that even if I *had* found out he'd loved another woman, or if Miss Summers *was* in love with somebody else, or if any of the other hundred and one awful possibilities that lurked around the corner *were* to happen, I could take it. It might knock me down temporarily, but it wouldn't put me out. Because I had guts. I was the one who had climbed up on the diving board in front of all my friends and jumped off into space. Alice the Brave, that was me.

When I got out to the bus stop, there was Elizabeth in her new jeans, the second button of her shirt undone. Alice the Brave and Elizabeth the Conqueror. We would take eighth grade by storm.

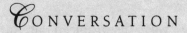CONVERSATION

*Y*ou know what's weird? When you're used to being one of the youngest, smallest, plainest kids in school, and suddenly you're an upper classman; you're one of the beautiful people.

Everywhere I looked there were younger kids running around looking worried, afraid they couldn't find their classrooms or work their locker combinations, or that there wouldn't be toilet paper in the johns. A lot of eighth-graders sent them in exactly the opposite direction if they asked where a classroom was, but mostly the younger kids didn't ask. Self-preservation, I guess.

I went out of my way to avoid Miss Summers's room. I didn't want to see her. Be reminded of her. Have her say anything to me, even. The really great thing was that I was in two different classes with Patrick and with almost everybody in health class—Pamela, Elizabeth, Patrick, Brian, and Mark, as well as Karen and Jill. If Tom Perona came to our school instead of St. John's, it would have been the whole gang. Of course Mark and Pamela were sitting on opposite sides of the room; Pamela was sitting with Brian, and Mark was flirting with every girl in sight to show Pamela he didn't care.

Everything was disorganized at lunchtime, and Elizabeth, Pamela, and I found ourselves sitting across the table from some eighth-grade boys we didn't know. They were kidding us about how they had this unusual ability to guess what kind of underwear girls were wearing. I could almost feel Elizabeth blushing before I even looked at her. I was all for ignoring them, when Pamela said, "Put up or shut up."

One of the boys grinned. "If we guess right, will you tell us?"

"Sure!" said Pamela, without even asking Elizabeth and me.

The boy in the Ohio State shirt looked right at Pamela. "Black bikini," he said.

"Purple," she told them.

"Pamela!" I whispered, nudging her. Couldn't she see this was all a trick to make us tell them what we were wearing?

But now they were looking at me and smiling. "What do you think?" the boy said to his friends.

"I'd guess she's wearing pants with the word 'Tuesday' on the seat," said one of his friends.

I stared. Actually, I was wearing pants with the word "Tuesday" printed all over them. Now I was blushing.

"Bingo!" they said, and laughed.

Elizabeth was drinking from her milk carton, eyes on the table, face as red as a tomato, when they turned to her.

"Cotton Jockies," said the boy in the sweatshirt, which is *exactly* the kind of pants Elizabeth wears.

She choked and spattered milk all over the table.

It was going to be an interesting year. —

There was an assembly that afternoon to introduce the new teachers and the cheerleaders and the presidents of the seventh- and eighth-grade classes.

Mr. Orman, our principal, got up to welcome the new seventh-graders to junior high, and the eight-graders back again. He explained the fire drills and the rules, he introduced the new teachers, the exchange teachers, and then he said he wanted to extend a special welcome to our new vice-principal, who had left our school as a math teacher to get a degree in administration, and was now back as our vice-principal–Mr. Jim Sorringer. We clapped.

Then Mr. Sorringer got up to say how glad he was to be here again in Silver Spring, and suddenly I was staring at his heavy eyelids and his craggy face and knew at once that's who Miss Summers had been having dinner with the night before.

I closed my eyes and began to smile. A business dinner, that's all it was! A conversation about curriculum! Miss Summers and Dad were safe. She would be my stepmother after all, and we would live happily ever after.

There was no *guarantee,* of course, but things certainly looked more promising.

"What are you grinning about?" Pamela whispered, poking me. She and Brian were sitting next to me, holding hands.

"The world is a great place after all," I said.

At dinner that night, we all talked about "our day." Dad said he didn't know what he was going to do about Loretta Jenkins, because she wasn't sure when the baby was due and hadn't seen a doctor yet. She wasn't exactly happy about having a baby, either.

Janice Sherman was recovering nicely, but seemed depressed when Dad talked to her on the phone.

"I've got it!" I said suddenly. "If Loretta doesn't want a baby, and Janice is depressed because she can't ever have one, why doesn't Loretta give her baby to Janice for adoption?" Some problems have such obvious solutions you wonder why adults don't think of them more often.

"Is that all you have to contribute?" asked Dad, and then I knew it wasn't such a hot idea.

Lester told us about how he was thinking of switching from business to philosophy for a major, because he was enjoying his philosophy courses so much.

"Have you thought just how you might support yourself with a degree in philosophy?" Dad asked.

"No sweat," said Lester. "I'll simply build a hut at the top of the Himalayas so people can make pilgrimages to the top and ask me the meaning of life."

Dad rolled his eyes, but then he and Lester both looked at me, waiting to hear about my day. I wanted to tell them about how the man Miss Summers had been out with was only our vice-principal, but I knew I couldn't say a word. So I told them about the eighth-grade boys who could guess what kind of underpants girls were wearing.

Dad leaned back in his chair with a sigh. "You know," he said, "it does seem that we could make a point of more stimulating conversations at mealtimes. It wouldn't hurt us a bit to be thinking of topics in advance that we could all discuss. Issues to debate. It could be anything at all—philosophy, music, religion, politics. I don't want you two going out into the world remembering dinner hour as just a big game of Trivial Pursuit."

"I *like* Trivial Pursuit," I said.

"Pass the catsup," said Lester.

For a while forks clinked, jaws chewed, bread was buttered, crackers snapped.

"I have a topic," I said at last.

"Good!" said Dad. "Let's hear it."

"I would like to know the definition of Cairene motitations," I told them.

"Of *what*?" Lester stared at me.

"Cairene motitations."

"Never heard of them," he said.

"We could look it up," said Dad. "How do you spell 'Cairene'?"

"What about Yemani wrigglings?" I knew those phrases by heart. Ever since Elizabeth told me to forget them, they were imprinted forever on my mind.

Dad studied me intently. Even Les looked fascinated.

"No?" I said. "What about Abyssinian sobbings, Nubian lasciviousness, or Upper Egyptian heat?"

Lester's mouth dropped, but Dad was beginning to smile.

"Has somebody been dipping into *Tales from the Arabian Nights,* by chance?" he asked. "Ah, yes! I spent many an evening with that book when I was about fourteen."

Then he and I began to laugh, and Lester joined in.

"Elizabeth was reading it to us one night on a sleep-over, but she felt so guilty she had to go to confession," I said. "I've never been able to get the stories out of my head."

"Tell you what, Dad," Lester said, grinning. "I'll look into Nubian lasciviousness if you'll take Upper Egyptian heat."

Dad smiled at me across the table. "Don't grow up too fast, Al. I like you just the way you are."

"I'll take it a day at a time," I promised.